D0729134

MURDER
IN THIN AIR

By Richard L. Baldwin

© Buttonwood Press 2008

This novel is a product of the imagination of the author. None of the events described in this story occurred. No characters in the story are intended to portray by description, personality, or behaviors those associated currently or in the past with Alma College or at the Battle Creek Balloon Festival. Many of the names in the story are actual names of students who attended Alma College with the author 1959-1962, but there is no intent to associate a name with a character of the imagination in this story. Though settings, buildings, businesses exist, liberties may have been taken as to actual locations and description. This story has no purpose other than to entertain the reader.

Published by Buttonwood Press
P.O. Box 716
Haslett, Michigan 48840
www.buttonwoodpress.com

ISBN: 978-0-9742920-9-0
Printed in the United States of America

I dedicate this book to my grandmother,
Maybelle Howard McMillan.

While I never met my maternal grandmother,
the stories of her creativity in music and art abound.
She attended Alma College at age 16,
and was a member of their music faculty for a short time
in the early years of the twentieth century.

OTHER BOOKS
BY RICHARD L. BALDWIN

FICTION:

A Lesson Plan for Murder (1998)
ISBN: 0-9660685-0-5. Buttonwood Press.

The Principal Cause of Death (1999)
ISBN: 0-9660685-2-1. Buttonwood Press.

Administration Can Be Murder (2000)
ISBN: 0-9660685-4-8. Buttonwood Press.

Buried Secrets of Bois Blanc: Murder in the Straits of Mackinac (2001)
ISBN: 0-9660685-5-6. Buttonwood Press.

The Marina Murders (2003)
ISBN: 0-9660685-7-2. Buttonwood Press.

A Final Crossing: Murder on the S.S. Badger (2004)
ISBN: 0-9742920-2-8. Buttonwood Press.

Poaching Man and Beast: Murder in the North Woods (2006)
ISBN: 0-9742920-3-6. Buttonwood Press.

The Lighthouse Murders (2007)
ISBN: 978-0-9742920-5-2. Buttonwood Press.

The Searing Mysteries: Three in One (2001)
ISBN: 0-9660685-6-4. Buttonwood Press.

Ghostly Links (2004)
ISBN: 0-9660685-8-0. Buttonwood Press.

The Moon Beach Mysteries (2003)
ISBN: 0-9660685-9-9. Buttonwood Press.

The Detective Company (2004; written with Sandie Jones.)
ISBN: 0-9742920-0-1. Buttonwood Press.

Unity and the Children (2000)
ISBN: 0-9660685-3-X. Buttonwood Press.

NON-FICTION:

If A Child Picked A Flower Just For You (2004)
Buttonwood Press

The Piano Recital (1999)
ISBN: 0-9660685-1-3. Buttonwood Press.

A Story to Tell: Special Education in Michigan's Upper Peninsula 1902-1975 (1994)
ISBN: 932212-77-8. Lake Superior Press.

Warriors and Special Olympics: The Wertz Warrior Story (2006)
ISBN: 0-9742920-4-4. Buttonwood Press, LLC.

ACKNOWLEDGEMENTS

I wish to thank Anne Ordiway, editor; Sarah Thomas, graphic designer and typesetter; Joyce Wagner, proofreader. Several people from Alma College were most helpful: President Saundra Tracy; Carol Hyble; and Michael Silverthorn. I also extend appreciation to Barbara Haluzska, Executive Director of Battle Creek's Field of Flight Air Show and Balloon Festival. I wish to thank Sherry Parker Skinner, Kathy Ornish, Dr. Karen Blackman, Jack Kelly, and Lt. Dave Kirk for their assistance. Finally, I thank Patty Baldwin for her support, her listening, her advice, and her love, without which this story and all the others I've written and published could have been told.

PLEASE SUPPORT

ALMA COLLEGE
www.almacollege.com

Alma College, located in the city of Alma in the middle of Michigan's Lower Peninsula, was founded in 1886 by a group of devoted Scottish Presbyterian clergy and laymen who had a dream: to establish a liberal arts college based upon the loftiest of ideals — unifying the human mind and spirit through knowledge. Today, Alma College is a nationally recognized private liberal arts college that engages students in a personalized education, encourages their pursuit of extraordinary achievements, and highlights the importance of social responsibility. More than 1,300 students annually pursue undergraduate degrees on the picturesque 125-acre campus. Alumni contribute to society in their roles as attorneys, physicians, teachers, scientists, entrepreneurs, communicators, performing artists and in many other professions.

BATTLE CREEK'S FIELD OF FLIGHT
AIR SHOW AND BALLOON FESTIVAL
www.bcballoons.com

The 2008 show will take place at the W.K. Kellogg Airport from July 2 through July 6. Please visit the festival website for information. The U.S. Air Force Thunderbirds are scheduled to appear and over 65 balloons are expected to fill the sky over the Cereal Capital of America, Battle Creek, Michigan.

ONE

October 1:
The Campus of Alma College, Alma, Michigan

That a murder might involve a professor of an elite, church-supported institution of higher learning was unconscionable. If a safe academic environment could be presumed, it would be at the eight Michigan colleges of the Michigan Intercollegiate Athletic Association: Adrian; Albion; Alma; Aquinas; Calvin; Hope; Kalamazoo; and Olivet. For many graduates around the country, seemingly endless tragedies had taken place at their beloved alma maters. But excellence can also meet evil in a setting where only the former should exist.

The life of an undergraduate student at a demanding college is stressful enough without having to face the prospect of never becoming the doctor, lawyer, corporate executive, or teacher assumed for him or her by family, friends, and commencement speakers. The transition from a valedictorian who received nothing lower than an A to a failure in a sophomore chemistry course was an unwelcome wake-up call.

At 8:00 a.m. on Friday, October 1, the first meeting following mid-term examinations in Chemistry 231, distinguished Visiting Professor Janet Reid returned the graded tests. As the students sat stunned staring at the letter grades in red ink, they heard their professor say, "Many of you should be disturbed with the results of this examination. I'm surprised you did so poorly. You were accepted at Alma College because you were high achievers at your high schools, the leaders of tomorrow. You're aiming for careers that could take law, medicine, and economics to new levels. Unfortunately, your performance on this examination doesn't reflect the expectation of excellence at Alma. The highest grade on this examination was a C-minus, earned by Sherry Parker. The rest of you received Ds and Es, meaning you are on the verge of not passing this course, lowering your GPA, and eventually jeopardizing your acceptance into graduate schools."

The students' facial expressions resembled those of mourners at a local mortuary. Two coeds discreetly dabbed tears. One young man abruptly left the class, apparently experiencing an anxiety attack. The remainder sat stoically, disbelieving what they had heard, while imagining their parents' faces as they reacted to such news.

As Dr. Reid surveyed the depression around the room, she realized that her students were in no frame of mind to discuss today's topic of covalent bonds between organic and inorganic substances, so she reluctantly dismissed the class. The students filed out of the room, wondering how best to alleviate stress. A couple of students walked to Dunning Memorial Chapel to pray.

Most of the students called their parents. News of what they considered their unfair mid-term grades took hold in the minds of loving parents who immediately sympathized with their sons or daughters. In some cases they shared tears; in others, parents voiced angry feelings. Responses ranged from, "Come on home for the weekend," to "I'll call the dean and get some answers!"

Most of the Chem 231 students went home to share their sorrow with family and friends. Visits to hometown high school football games and dances would bring back positive memories of excellent grades and much less stress than what they now faced in college.

Dr. Janet Reid was an academician of the highest order, having graduated from Detroit's Cass Technical High School, a prestigious secondary school, before earning a chemistry degree from M.I.T. She was a member of the swimming team at M.I.T., and through that experience realized how demanding the life of a student athlete could be; there simply weren't enough hours in the day to excel as both a student and as an athlete.

After obtaining advanced degrees in chemistry from Boston College, Janet was first hired by Yale University. She had later moved to Lake Superior State University in Michigan, and then on to Alma, as part of Alma's plan to graduate the brightest and most gifted minds in the Midwest.

Dr. Reid was a loner. She found no time for a relationship, let alone marriage, so she had "married" her passion for chemistry and teaching. She had spent more time writing scientific manuscripts and reviewing articles for journals than many people spend with their spouses and families. Though consumed by her academic passion, she was a woman with compassion for highly-gifted chemistry majors who were also athletes.

Late Friday afternoon, Dr. Reid gathered things in her office and prepared to stop briefly at her apartment. She was on her way to Battle Creek to compete in the annual national championship balloon festival. Her balloon Bagpiper was entered in most of the events. She planned to meet her chase crew in the early evening for dinner and looked forward to seeing many friends at the event.

As Janet glanced out her window onto the Alma College campus, she reflected on earlier comments to her students and the devastating effect they appeared to have had. Maybe her "gloom and doom" speech had been too strong. Perhaps she had unnecessarily panicked the young minds. But, what's done is done, she thought. Much of college life is adjustment: to independence, to interaction with a variety of people, to acceptance of responsibility.

On her way out of the lab adjoining her office, she checked the fume hood to see that burners were off, chemicals put away, and that the gas and water pipes were emptied and safe. With her arms laden with papers, a large briefcase, a tote bag, and a folder fat with information about the balloon festival, she didn't notice when a strap from her brief case hooked onto the electric hot-plate controls, turning the power knob slightly to "on." She tugged the strap free, walked out of her office, locked the door, and was on her way to Battle Creek.

Unbeknownst to Janet, an acetone bottle in the fume hood had also tipped over, dislodging its stopper. The liquid flowed across the stone hard floor, dripping onto the tile floor of the lab. The hood filled with vapor while the acetone formed a trail into her adjoining office.

Late Friday afternoon, Father McDonald sat in the confessional at St. James Catholic Church in Alma. He wasn't really expecting anyone to visit: he usually brought a William Kienzle mystery with him to pass the time. Contrary to what people might think, he didn't enjoy this part of being a priest. Penitents were usually uncomfortable during confession, and he often heard a sad commentary on life. People sure make bad decisions that lead to heartache and conflict, he reflected. But hearing confessions was a part of his job, and he hoped that freeing his flock from guilt was truly a blessing. He sometimes explained to people, especially Protestants, that the sacrament of confession went back to Jesus's telling his apostles that they are to forgive sin. But Jesus didn't say they had to like the process, and Father McDonald didn't.

Father was well into *The Rosary Murders* when he heard the door to the penitent's cubicle shut. "Father, forgive me, for I have sinned. My last confession was about three months ago." The voice was only a whisper, and Father strained to hear the words.

"Tell me the nature of your sin," Father responded.

"I plan to kill a college professor. I am truly sorry, but it needs to be done. Lives are being ripped apart, and that needs to stop. I asked the president to intervene, but she wouldn't. I know I'll go to hell for breaking a commandment, but I'm hoping you'll understand."

Father McDonald could hear quiet sobbing in the cubicle. "Have you told the authorities about this?"

"No. I can't. I mean, I can — but no, I can't. Everyone I know would be shocked and devastated." There was a brief pause. "I needed to tell someone, and I know you can't repeat this to anyone."

"Even though you have not committed the murder at this point, you have harbored evil thoughts, separating you from God. The fact that you are here is in itself an act of contrition. You seek God's forgiveness, but I urge you to rethink your plan and perhaps to seek counseling. Can I help you find a therapist or counselor?"

"Oh, no, I can't tell anyone but you. I'll only kill once, Father, but it is justified."

"No, the taking of a life is not justified. Humans can't make those decisions, nor can they take a life."

"But it has to stop — it simply has to." The whisper was almost inaudible. "She's evil and plays God."

"I understand you believe that, but in a civilized society and as Christians, we need to resolve injustices in ways other than murder."

"Well, I'm sorry, but I'm going to do it."

"Please pray with me," Father began. "Lord God, please send your spirit of Love to guide your child. Troubling thoughts are clouding the commandment to love one another. Please allow love to temper this person's thinking and to erase a plan of harming another of your children. We ask this in the name of your son, Jesus Christ. Amen."

"I don't understand your judging my thinking, Father. I'm striking out at Satan. I thought you would be understanding and compassionate and healing."

"I am all those. I want to help you get some professional care for your angry feelings, and I want to protect this professor from death." There was an uncomfortable pause. Then Father said, "Pray to ask forgiveness of your sinful thoughts and your plan to take another's life."

Father could only hear mumbling and when it stopped, he said, "Your sins are forgiven. Your penance is to read the commandments and to read the words of Jesus Christ when one of his disciples used violence as Jesus was being arrested by the Roman soldiers. Finally, I ask that you get some help for your anger so you can channel your hatred into a more acceptable plan of action. May God bless you, in the name of the Father, the Son, and the Holy Spirit."

Father McDonald heard what sounded like "Thank you, Father." The door to the confessional opened as the penitent left quickly, muttering words that were not discernable. Father thought about opening his door to see who had just visited, but he thought better of the idea. Returning to his novel, he found himself totally distracted. He was now trapped in secrecy, for he could not tell anyone of this impending crisis. He couldn't seek guidance from the Bishop or another priest. In his heart, he knew that a professor was in harm's way, and he was helpless in his role of guarding and protecting the soul of a child of God. He prayed that there would be no murder involving a professor on Alma's campus, lest he be overcome with guilt for not doing something to intervene. But he could not act because the nature of confession and repentance is a trust-filled event between the confessor and the priest.

TWO

October 2:
Alma College, Alma, Michigan

The alarm sounded at 1:23 a.m. in Dow Science Center on the Alma College campus, just west of Alma, Michigan. The campus night security detail immediately responded, as did the Alma City Fire Department. Red beams of light cut through the quiet fall night like lasers from a carnival light-show. When firefighters arrived, smoke poured from a first-floor window, and flames were visible inside the building. The firefighters moved with precision, entered the building, and with expert firefighting, soon had the blaze under control.

Only a handful of students, no doubt pulling weekend all-nighters, ventured into the cold to watch the action on campus. The excitement was a welcome break from routine.

A fireman reported to the Chief that no one was in the building and that chemicals that could have caused additional explosions or damage were secure. It was not yet clear how the fire started. No one would be allowed to enter the building until the state fire inspector had completed his analysis of the fire, which meant Dow classes were canceled until Tuesday at least.

Before the fire was fully contained, President Elizabeth Shanks was on the scene talking with the fire chief and her director of campus safety. The three watched as the office and adjoining lab of chemistry professor Janet Reid were consumed by flames. President Shanks immediately recalled the 1969 fire in Old Main, but that disaster had consumed the entire building, and fortunately this fire had not done extensive damage. The alarm system in the science building was state-of-the-art, and the sprinkler system had nearly controlled the flames before water came in from fire hoses.

President Shanks, the twelfth president of Alma College since 1887, was tall, attractive, and seemed always to be clad in appropriate business attire. She had earned a Ph.D. in Public Policy from Princeton in 1990, and had been awarded a Doctor of Divinity degree from Princeton Theological Seminary in 1995. She was a decisive leader and an excellent fund-raiser. She valued Alma's exceptional students and admired its faculty, impressively credentialed people who put learning above publishing, while continuing to support research. She knew that one mark of a prestigious college was deep pockets filled with grants from the government and private corporations, money designated to populate a future with compassionate, healthy, and intellectual citizens.

President Shanks retired to her office where she composed a notice to be posted in dorms and on outside doors of Dow Science Center. She also prepared a press release, called the members of the Board of Regents to inform them of events, called her administrative team, and then notified Dr. Lou Economeau, the Chair of the Science Department.

Saturday's sunrise on a clear fall day would reveal a black gap on Alma's campus. Fortunately, insurance should cover the fire damage and it appeared that beyond one chemistry lab, one faculty office, and some adjacent water damage, the building was intact.

The question remained: Was it arson or accident? Would more fires break out on campus, or was this an isolated incident? Following breakfast, President Shanks called a meeting of her administrative team, chairpersons of all departments, residence hall directors, and campus security. She wanted to review emergency procedures, establish a heightened sense of concern, and hear reports of anything seen or overheard that might explain the fire in the Dow Science Center and avert possible future damage.

By the luck of the MIAA schedule, the week's football game with Hope College was being played in Holland. Many students had gone home, for this was the weekend after mid-term exams, and nothing of significance was scheduled on campus. Had this been Homecoming weekend, the campus would have been buzzing with reunions, a parade, football game, dance, and banquets. A fire on campus was bad news on any day, but if one had to occur, this was a better day than many.

THREE

October 2:
Battle Creek Field of Flight Air Show and Balloon Festival,
Battle Creek, Michigan

Planting a bomb in the wicker basket of a hot air balloon could not have been easier. There was minimal field security at the Battle Creek Hot Air Balloon Festival. As pilots and crews laid the baskets on their sides and straightened the rip-stop nylon envelope material in anticipation of hot air filling the balloon, a figure with a definite purpose walked among the spectators who were enjoying seeing the pilots up close. Within the hour, the balloons would rise, seemingly effortlessly, into the early morning skies over America's Cereal City.

A shadowy figure placed the bomb in a certain basket between the wicker and one of its four propane tanks, each containing ten gallons of fuel, enough to heat the trapped air so that the balloon could stay airborne for about two hours. None of the spectators took note as the person knelt by the basket, reached in, and positioned the small bomb. The pilot and crew had nearly finished laying out the seventy-foot-long craft from the bottom of the basket to the top of envelope. Even if a spectator noticed a person entering a basket during preparation for lift-off, it was not cause for concern, unless the pilot noticed, and in this case, the pilot was straightening the balloon material several yards from the basket.

The bomb contained an altitude sensor set for 2000 feet. Detonation would puncture the propane tank and the subsequent explosions would cause the basket and its contents to disintegrate in mid-air.

The balloon, depending on the wind, would no doubt rise with the heat of the explosion, falling to earth eventually as the air within the balloon cooled.

Once the bomb was planted, the intruder quickly but calmly moved away from Janet Reid's balloon. An observer might become suspicious, or a camera could inadvertently catch an image of the soon-to-be murderer.

The first event was called the Hare and the Hounds. The "hare," an official's balloon, was launched with a fifteen-minute head start on the contestants. The hare's pilot would drop an X-target for the "hounds" who would follow, attempting to drop a weighted bag closest to the large X, thereby winning the event. When given the signal to start, Janet Reid and about forty other balloonists fired up their burners providing ten million BTUs to heat the 70,000 cubic feet of air, lifting the envelopes into the sky like marionettes rising from a stage.

Dr. Janet Reid was a professional balloonist who competed in events all over North America. Janet's balloon was an audience-pleaser named the Bagpiper, reflecting Alma's rich Scottish heritage. The nylon resembled a tartan plaid with an attractive mixture of greens, reds, and browns. Fabric "pipes" of the bagpipe protruded from the teardrop envelope.

On this chilly October morning, spectators watched in awe as one by one, multicolored balloons began to rise, and "hounds" chased the "hare," hoping to ride wind currents to be able to drop their weighted bags onto the huge X. Coming closest to the X meant victory, earning not only status, but also a monetary gift or a trophy, which signified piloting luck and skill.

Janet piloted the Bagpiper over the trees; it truly looked like a flying Scottish bagpipe. Her chase crew, Linda Ross, Barry Sims, and Pat True, climbed into Janet's Suburban and began to follow the balloon's path, using roads that led in an easterly direction. Barry contacted Janet by radio to make sure the two-way communication system was working properly. There would not be much chit-chat, for Janet was busy planning her flight, regulating the flames below the belly of the balloon to control its lift.

Janet kept an eye on the altimeter. She couldn't use technology to chart a course because she was at the mercy of the ten-to-fifteen-mile-an-hour breeze. But like any good pilot, she wanted all the data at her disposal, and knowing her altitude met that expectation. On occasion she glanced at her variometer to verify whether she was ascending or descending.

The other balloons were lifting off, a few at a time, careful not to come too close to other competitors. This competition was not a race, so quick ascent was not an advantage. When you were ready to lift, you did so, always respectful of other pilots near you.

People watching the lifts were jealous that they were not along for the ride and could only marvel at the beauty of the colorful envelopes floating in mid-air. The murderer, watching in a pickup truck a few miles east of the lift area, felt like a child at Fourth of July fireworks. There was no telling just when the Bagpiper might reach 2000 feet, kill Janet Reid, and give spectators a catastrophic vision they would never forget.

Janet checked her altimeter — 1850 feet. She decided to fly a contour flight-plan, an up-and-down pattern, while being pushed along by the slight wind. When the balloon reached 1850, Janet decided to forget the contour patterning and rise, then descend as she approached the target. She gripped the valve controlling the flames that heated the balloon air. With each three-second burst of flame, the balloon lifted a bit. Janet hoped she would have an advantage, since all of her competitors were still contouring. The balloon continued to rise as the wind nudged the craft toward the target where she would carefully drop the weighted bag, assuring another victory.

Janet took a moment to marvel at the scenery. The sunrise was exquisite — it seemed the earth and its inhabitants were awaking to the perfect day. At 1900 feet, Janet pondered whether she was high enough to descend to the target or whether she needed a bit more altitude.

Janet decided she could descend faster from a higher altitude, so she chose to take the balloon to 2200 feet. From this look-out point, the murderer began to think that Janet Reid wouldn't meet her Maker on this particular day after all. None of the other balloons were rising, and Janet was still visible in the morning sky hovering over Ceresco, a few miles southeast of Battle Creek.

The altimeter read 1980 feet as Janet gripped the burner control, squeezed it, and heated the balloon air for three more seconds. In the Suburban, the driver of the chase crew, Linda Ross, picked up the radio to communicate with Janet. She never made contact.

At 2000 feet, the bomb triggered an explosion in one of the propane tanks. The tank's shrapnel punctured the remaining tanks, sending released propane into the burner flame. The result was reminiscent of the space shuttle Columbia when it exploded in 2003. Janet never knew that death was imminent, nor suffered any pain, for the blast took her life in an instant. The basket flew apart, raining debris onto a wheat field below. Released from its weight, the balloon continued to ride the wind currents because of the hot air trapped inside.

"It's done. Mission accomplished," the murderer said out loud to no one in the pickup. As the key in the ignition turned, thoughts struck, "That was easier than shooting a duck out of the sky. Sick as it sounds, it was actually a beautiful sight. And I think I've pulled off the perfect crime. There will be no evidence at the scene, no clue for the police. Now, students can get on with their lives."

Pat True, a member of Janet Reid's chase crew, called 911 as the Suburban sped toward the field where pieces of the basket had fallen. Other witnesses had called 911 as well. The chase crew knew they could do nothing and did not want to see wreckage close-up, so they stayed back to guide emergency vehicles and to talk to the police. They stood helpless in shock and disbelief as they experienced a tragedy beyond explanation.

The farmer, Anthony Taylor, in whose field the debris landed, had observed the destruction first-hand. It was his annual tradition to invite neighbors over for the balloon race on this first Saturday in October and most of the guests were outside watching the balloons. Drawing on his home emergency plan, he directed his guests where to move so that emergency vehicles could easily enter the property. He then set about securing his livestock so there would be no need to round up panicked animals. Instinctively, farmer Taylor understood what would be happening with emergency vehicles, the sheriff and deputies, the media, close friends and relatives; hence he was able to calmly direct operations.

And, it happened as Anthony expected. The police, state police, Calhoun County Sheriff Mike Pritchard and his deputies locked down a four-square-mile area. A Federal Aviation Agency crew was dispatched to the scene.

EMTs quickly confirmed that Janet Reid had no heartbeat then left her body covered with a blanket for the medical examiner who would soon be on the scene.

Witnesses seemed in agreement that just before the explosion, they had seen a bright flash from the side of the basket, then heard an explosion. The disaster area was actually an organized frenzy with each professional carrying out his or her job, as practiced in numerous post-9/11 disaster-training drills.

The FAA investigators quickly discerned a possible criminal element in the accident and brought in the county sheriff. The FAA would continue the search for aeronautic causes, write a long and detailed report, and announce their findings after the report was approved by superiors.

Presently, media trucks appeared, hoisted antennas, and conducted live broadcasts from near the scene. Mr. Taylor had the good sense to call the county emergency response team so counseling could begin immediately for friends and relatives shocked by the disaster.

Linda, Barry and Pat were in a state of shock. Between sobs they tried to answer questions about the accident, but they had no answers. Janet had simply been piloting the Bagpiper toward the target downwind. No, she hadn't given any indication of concern. No, they knew of no one who might want Janet dead. Yes, the craft had been inspected, and all equipment had been approved. They had no explanation for the nightmare they were suddenly living.

Word of the explosion quickly spread as pilots alerted their chase crews to what they had observed from the air. Balloons immediately began to descend as pilots searched out safe places to land. There was no panic, but it was clear that this might not be an isolated incident. If it was the work of terrorists or a serial killer, other explosions could occur at any second. Caution was the by-word.

Linda, Barry, and Pat were checked out by paramedics before they talked with the county emergency response team. Suffering nothing other than intensive grief and high blood pressure, they were cleared to leave the area. Linda offered to drive the crew back to the festival; in their conversation on the way back, they tried to cope with and explain the inexplicable.

The medical examiner arrived, certified the death, and released the body, which was then put in a labeled evidence body-bag and placed in a hearse from a local funeral home. The vehicle slowly made its way through an army of response personnel and vehicles before finding an exit, then headed toward Battle Creek, carrying the remains of one who moments earlier had believed herself to be in Heaven watching the birth of a new day. Within a half hour, the hearse would arrive at the county morgue; the body would be brought in and prepared for autopsy.

FOUR

The Home of Lou and Carol Searing,
Grand Haven, Michigan

Approaching 70 years of age, Lou Searing had retired in 1997 after more than thirty years of teaching children and college students and serving as Michigan's Director of Special Education. His avocation over the previous ten years had been assisting authorities in murder investigations and then writing a book about each case. Lou usually thought of himself as "practically" — practically bald, practically deaf, and practically forgetful — but now he was an investigator with a good reputation, as well as a writer with a following. Life was good.

Carol Searing, Lou's "better half," as a friend always referred to her, had brought love, patience, and companionship to the past 35 years of his life. Carol was gracefully approaching her 70th birthday, but most people would never suspect it. Her face was angelic and her personality loving and caring. Lou felt he was truly blessed to share life with Carol, their golden retriever Samm, and their cat Millie, both of whom were also getting on in years.

The Searing home on the shore of Lake Michigan south of Grand Haven was a gift to each other following their retirements from careers in special education. Lou could investigate crime and write books about the experiences. Carol could quilt in her studio, volunteer at the Ronald McDonald House, and dote on the eight

Searing grandchildren — four Searings in Grand Rapids, and four Hoffmeisters in St. Louis.

Each evening, in good weather, Lou and Carol walked along the shore. Their golden retriever, Samm, disabled from a rifle shot a couple of years before, often rode behind them in her red "Flyer" wagon, wishing she could chase the sea gulls or a driftwood stick, but enjoying the jaunt.

Each summer, the grandchildren came to Grand Haven for time with Grandpa and Nana. They spent the better part of each day on the beach, swimming, playing with Frisbees and footballs. For now, the kids were confined to the home and beach front. Lou and Carol enjoyed having the children to themselves, for they knew teen-age freedom as well as boy and girl friends would soon "take" the grandkids from them. Their worlds would expand into town and out into the Lake, with boats, cars, and skidoos.

Lou was watching The CBS Saturday Early Show when suddenly, show host Russ Mitchell announced, "The small town of Alma, Michigan, home of Alma College, is saddened today by the death of Dr. Janet Reid, a visiting professor of chemistry. Dr. Reid's hot air balloon exploded early this morning during the Battle Creek Field of Flight Air Show and Balloon Festival. Dr. Elizabeth Shanks, president of Alma, expressed shock and sadness at Dr. Reid's death. Alma College, a Presbyterian-supported four-year institution, is home to sixteen hundred students from throughout the country and the world. Local law enforcement and the Federal Aviation Authority are investigating."

Lou was shocked to hear this news. A student at Alma College from 1959 to 1962, he had been on the golf team, a member of Tau Kappa Epsilon fraternity, the Kiltie Marching Band, and the debate team. He had enrolled at Alma in preparation for the Presbyterian ministry but had transferred to Western Michigan University to pursue his interest in special education, a specialty not offered at Alma.

Following the newscast and Russ's farewell comment, the phone rang in the Searing home. It was the president of Alma College, Dr. Elizabeth Shanks.

"You've probably heard of the tragedy we've suffered, Lou."

"Yes, I caught it on the news."

"We are all stunned; we cannot explain this." Dr. Shanks paused. "The Calhoun County sheriff thinks Dr. Reid was murdered."

"I can only imagine the upset on your campus, Dr. Shanks," Lou replied sympathetically.

"Yes, it's disturbing, to say the least. I'm calling to ask if you would apply your skills to help solve this mystery."

"It's kind of you to call, and I'd be happy to help out. My parents graduated from Alma in 1932, my grandmother McMillan graduated and taught there in the early 1900s, and I attended Alma for a couple of years around 1960."

"Yes, we know our distinguished alumni well, Lou, and you are among them."

"Nice of you to say, but first, I'm not a graduate, and second, when I consider the graduates who have gone on to greater things, I hardly fit into that crowd."

"You're a humble man, Lou. Regardless, we need to solve this quickly, to forestall potential damage to our reputation, fund-raising, and recruiting. You can't imagine the ripple effect this kind of publicity will have."

"Oh, yes, I can," Lou said. "Okay. If the sheriff concludes that this professor was murdered, I'll give it my best. As I understand that it hasn't been confirmed yet. And, the responsible office to investigate the murder has to invite or allow me to work on the case…"

"I understand. God bless you, Lou. Thank you so much."

"Also, if I work on the case, my assistant, Jack Kelly, will join me. I trust that's agreeable?"

"Do whatever you need to do, bring whomever you need to bring. Whatever I can do to arrange interviews, access to the campus — you need only ask."

Mid-morning Lou gazed at the magnificent blue sky and water from his writing studio on the second floor. He was thinking of Alma College and his promise to work a difficult case when he heard the phone ring.

Carol answered this second call while sorting fat quarters in her quilting studio. She leaned in the door to Lou's office saying, "It's Jack Kelly, for you." Jack, an accountant, retired from Gospel Communications in Muskegon, Michigan, had been Lou's assistant in his last case, which he had documented in The Lighthouse Murders. He was a tall and distinguished-looking gentleman with a carefully-trimmed goatee.

Lou picked up his phone. "Hi, Jack. What's up?"

"You've heard about the ballooning explosion this morning?"

"Yes. I saw it on the news," Lou replied. "Tragic."

"Have you heard of the professor?" Jack asked.

"No. I may have seen her name in an Alma publication, but I never met her. She was a visiting chemistry professor, as I recall."

"That's my understanding. I am sure it's a great loss to the college," Jack replied sympathetically. "I wonder if she had a family."

"For their sake, I certainly hope not," Lou replied.

"I think we should look into this," Jack suggested.

Lou replied, "Alma's president asked me already. I told her that we'll investigate under two conditions: first, it had to have been murder; and second, I needed to be accepted by the responsible law enforcement agency."

"I see," Jack replied. "They will be calling you, because it must have been a murder. A balloonist, peacefully floating along, and the balloon explodes? What else could it be?"

"For starters, a gas leak," Lou reasoned.

"Logical," Jack admitted. "I won't tie up your phone, my friend."

"OK. Thanks for calling, Jack."

Lou put the phone on the cradle as Carol appeared at his office door again. "What did Jack want?" Carol asked.

"A balloonist died this morning at the Hot Air Balloon Festival in Battle Creek. Jack thinks the pilot was murdered, but I'm not so sure."

"I see." Carol was always leery of Lou becoming involved with murder investigations. "And you're going to be involved if Jack is right?"

"I assured President Shanks I would help, but I need to be invited to participate by the law enforcement agency responsible for investigating the crime."

When the phone rang a third time, Lou answered.

"Mr. Searing? This is Mike Pritchard, Calhoun County Sheriff."

"I take it the balloonist was murdered?" Lou asked, jumping ahead.

"We think so. Can I count on you and Mr. Kelly to help us?"

"Yes, I'll help. But, how did you know to call me?" Lou asked.

"Jack Kelly. He says you're the best in the business, and I think this case will be a tough nut to crack."

"Did Jack contact you, or the other way around?" Lou asked.

"I called Alma College for information about the victim. Dean Atkins told me about Jack, said he was on campus for a lecture on restaurant operation. I understand he has a well-known eatery up near Manistee. The dean said this Mr. Kelly worked with you on your last case."

"Yes, that's right. Jack's very good. I call him Sancho, like the character in Man of LaMancha. He doesn't want to chase windmills; he just wants to tend the horse, shine shoes, and help me, like Sancho helped Don Quixote."

"Every sheriff could use a few Sanchos."

"I'll talk to Jack, we'll come down and talk to you, and then we'll decide what to do. I take it the medical examiner gave you an obvious cause of death. But do you have suspects, or motive?"

"No," Sheriff Pritchard replied.

"We'll likely see you yet this afternoon, say around three o'clock"

"Thanks, Mr. Searing."

"Please call me Lou, okay, Sheriff?"

"Thanks, Lou."

Jack drove to Grand Haven, picked up Lou, and the two headed for Battle Creek. On the way, they talked about a variety of subjects, getting caught up on each other's families, plans for upcoming holidays, and the news of the week. They parked in a visitor's spot at the county complex of offices, entered the sheriff's office, asked for Sheriff Pritchard, and sat down to wait for the receptionist's invitation to enter his office.

"Sheriff Pritchard will see you now, gentlemen." The two rose and followed the receptionist into the office. Sheriff Pritchard was of slight build, well-groomed, and middle-aged. He didn't look threatening, but Lou noticed a number of judo awards on his office wall.

"Mr. Searing, Mr. Kelly, thank you for coming down." Sheriff Pritchard extended his hand to shake theirs.

"Our pleasure, actually," Lou replied.

"Well, it is my pleasure. With you two on the case, I trust we'll wrap it up in short order."

"What do you have for us"? Lou asked. "We're ready to start."

Sheriff Pritchard opened a thin file folder. "The victim is Janet Reid, Doctor Janet Reid to be respectful, 43 years old, no family, visiting chemistry professor at Alma College in Alma, Michigan. She won national ballooning championships in her spare time. As a professor, she was strict, conservative, and maintained high academic standards. From what I've heard, she was respected by her bright students and hated by her less-than-serious students.

"Any suspects?" Jack asked.

"We've not identified any yet."

"Could there be a jealous balloonist?" Lou surmised. "A disgruntled student? Someone involved with a skeleton in her closet?"

"All are possible, Lou," the sheriff replied.

"Exactly what killed the professor?" Jack asked.

"Had to have been trauma from the blast," the sheriff said. "The autopsy is scheduled for Monday, but I'm not sure when the complete pathologist's report will be ready."

"Can we inspect the basket and balloon?" Lou asked.

"All you'll find is bits and pieces. We have the balloon stretched out in a hangar at the Cereal City Airport. The basket, propane tank, and burner were virtually destroyed. You can see what we've collected at your convenience."

"After this meeting would be fine."

"Okay. Anything else I can help you with?" Sheriff Pritchard asked.

"Do you have a detective assigned to this case, or will Lou and I be primary investigators?" Jack asked.

"One of my detectives has been assigned — Deputy Bob Jaggers. He is a no-nonsense guy with a lot of experience. He knows I've asked for your assistance, and he doesn't feel threatened by your involvement."

"Good, we'd like to talk with him."

"I'll give you his card and let him know you'll contact him."

The sheriff's phone rang. "Excuse me, please." Lou nodded.

"Sheriff Pritchard." As he listened, he glanced at Lou and Jack.

"Not a problem. I'm meeting with Mr. Searing and Mr. Kelly." He paused.

"Thanks. Lou and Jack will be contacting you. Keep up the good work, Deputy." Sheriff Pritchard hung up the phone and looked to Lou.

"The balloonist professor recently failed a number of students at Alma College," Sheriff Pritchard summarized what he had just learned about the failed mid-term exam. "Word on campus is that students in the class were demoralized by their exam grades and were quite angry. Dean John Atkins has promised full cooperation."

"We'll need to know who was in that class," Lou stated.

"Deputy Jaggers has already requested a class list. Students are definitely suspects."

"One of many possible leads," Lou replied.

"There's another event to consider. Professor Reid's office at Alma was torched, either late Friday night or very early Saturday morning. All of her records were destroyed — her office and an adjoining lab in Dow Science Center are gone. The fire department saved the building but nothing in her office was salvageable."

"Connected activities, maybe," Jack replied. "Perhaps the murderer didn't want something found."

"Grade reports, possibly," Lou added. "Thanks, Sheriff. We'd like to see the balloon, basket pieces, and other debris."

"I'll call the airport and authorize you to enter. Please wear gloves so you don't compromise the evidence."

"A given, Sheriff. Thanks for meeting with us."

"Thank you for coming down and offering to help."

"Our pleasure, "Lou replied. "Having your full cooperation and the willingness of Deputy Jaggers to work on this with us is appreciated."

"Thank you, Lou. One more thing for your information: while you were on your way to meet with me, I called the Gratiot County Sheriff and the Alma Chief of Police. Each has been briefed on the accident and suspicion of criminal activity. We three agreed that my office will conduct the investigation with the full support by the Alma-area-law enforcement agencies. They know you and Mr. Kelly will be investigating on my behalf. So, even though you'll be work-ing in the Alma area, within the jurisdiction of Gratiot County or the city of Alma, it's our case for solving."

"Thanks for the clarification, Sheriff. When I'm in someone else's sandbox, it's good to know that I have permission."

In the hangar of the Battle Creek Airport, Lou and Jack inspect-ed the remains of the wicker basket and its contents. The basket had a hole the size of a basketball and most of the thick wicker material was charred and appeared shredded. They noticed nothing out of the ordinary, realizing they actually had little sense of the ordinary.

The initial report from the FAA noted the burner had been inspected before the event and had been found to be functioning properly afterward. There were no bullet holes or other evidence that the balloon or the basket had been fired upon. Jack took some digital photos of basket-remains. Other than getting a close look at the debris, they gained little from their visit except a sense of awe at the result of an explosion.

On their way back to Grand Haven, the two men talked of peripheral things as well as specific plans for the investigation.

"Have you ever been up in a balloon, Jack?" Lou asked.

"No. It's something I think I'd like to do, but no, not yet."

"Me, neither. I think we had better get the experience," Lou said. "Are you game?"

"If you think it'll help us, I'm ready."

"Would Elaine like to go?" Lou asked Jack. If so, he'd ask Carol, and the four of them could have a unique experience.

"Ah, as well as I know Elaine, I think she'd want to watch from terra firma," Jack replied. "Would Carol want to go up?"

"I imagine she will. Flying doesn't bother her, and this is just floating a few hundred feet off the ground."

"When we get home, I'll ask Elaine. You ask Carol and we'll see if we have a foursome."

"Let's get back to the investigation," Lou suggested. "I'll call Detective Jaggers and arrange to talk to Janet's chase crew."

"And we want to see a class list for the students Janet Reid failed on that chemistry exam," Jack added.

"Right. We'll also want to talk to the head of the balloon festival to see whether there's reason to suspect anyone in that association."

"Looks like we've got our work cut out for us," Jack said, rubbing his hands together, anxious to get to work.

"Janet had no family as I understand it," Lou reasoned. "But some- one wanted her dead — of that we can be certain. And, that someone had a motive for his or her actions. We need to dig into her life to find someone who felt strongly enough about her to murder her."

"It sounds simple, but it never is."

"We'll handle it," Lou replied confidently. "It may be like finding a needle in the proverbial haystack, but we'll come upon it."

"Or, it might be fairly easy," Jack mused, "so I'm predicting a knitting needle in the haystack instead."

Jack Kelly answered his cell phone.

"Hi, Jack, Deputy Bob Jaggers here. I tried to call Lou but he didn't answer. Got a minute?"

"Sure, go ahead."

"The sheriff has suggested that we work as a trio rather than my acting alone and you and Lou working together. He thinks the coordination would be helpful."

"I think I can speak for Lou in saying we agree."

"I don't think we all need to be in on every interview, but we should share information and decide who will do what."

"Makes sense. How about our scheduling a conference call?"

"Good idea. You have my number, right?" Deputy Jaggers asked.

"Yes, we do."

"Give me a call when it's convenient for the two of you."

"Will do. Thanks for calling, Detective."

Sunday was quiet. Lou and Carol attended St. Patrick's Catholic Church in Grand Haven and sat in their accustomed pew at nine a.m. mass. The scripture reading, Romans 12:18-20, seemed to fit the mess Lou was about to encounter. "Do not take revenge, my friends, but leave room for God's wrath, for it is written: 'It is mine to avenge; I will repay,' says the Lord."

At coffee and donuts following mass, a couple of friends, Marilyn and Ken Malkowski joined them at a table. "I hear your alma mater has a crisis on its hands, Lou," Ken said.

"Yes. Post-9/11, every crime is automatically perceived to be the work of terrorists, and that's the fear of every college president and board of trustees. Every time something negative happens on a campus, a thousand presidents say in unison, 'There, but for the grace of God, go I.'"

Late Monday morning, Dr. Shanks' administrative secretary put before her a summary of the fire marshal's report. "I know you'll want to see this."

The report was extensive, but President Shanks was pleased to read the summary:

"After extensive review of the first floor fire in the Dow Science Center, I conclude that the fire was an accident. The door to the office/lab was locked, as were all doors to the Dow facility itself. A melted electric hot-plate was on the floor in front of the hood, probably dislodged from the hood by items falling in the course of the fire and its suppression. The hot-plate heated chemicals which spilled onto the counter, and the heating element ignited their vapors; the fire then spread from the lab into the office. There is no definitive evidence of arson. A review of security cameras at entrances to the Dow Center show no person entered after doors were locked at ten p.m. In sum, I declare the cause of the fire to be accidental, being caused by an electrical hot-plate igniting chemicals, most likely acetone vapor, the container of which was found on its side (without a stopper) near the hot-plate."

President Shanks breathed a sigh of relief. Any fire is tragic, but this one wasn't arson, so she needn't fear a student or faculty member causing more destruction. She directed that a copy of the report be given to Lou when he visited campus.

~~~

Murder was rare in the city of Alma and completely unheard of on the campus. The local police and the county sheriff had practically no experience in murder investigations. Police Chief John Worthington had always spent time praying — literally — that murder never occurred during his watch. And, if it should happen, he hoped the murderer could be found and convicted with minimal investigation, and with little question of guilt.

Now the chief faced a murder that was anything but simple. He was thankful that Lou Searing would lead the investigation. It would be a tough case, for there were no suspects, and no leads — only a dead Ph.D and eleven students relieved that the woman who had failed them on a mid-term was not around to sign a grading sheet.

Investigation of the murder was the Calhoun County sheriff's responsibility since the murder occurred within that jurisdiction, but Chief Worthington knew public perception of responsibility would be on his shoulders, because Dr. Reid had been a professor on the campus in his city.

SIX

October 4:
Office of Dr. Kirk Chandler,
Chair of the Communications Department, Albion College

"This meeting of the planning committee for the annual conference debate competition is called to order," said Kirk Chandler. "For the record, our secretary, Dr. Judy Molyneux, will poll the members for attendance.

"Dr. Molyneux, Calvin College."

"I'm obviously present," Judy chuckled,

"Dr. Margot Phelps, Hope College."

"Present."

"Ms. Julie Ruegsegger, Kalamazoo College."

"Excused," offered Dr. Chandler.

"Dr. Paul Voelker, Olivet College."

"Present."

"Dr. Charles Christian, Adrian College."

"Present."

"Thank you. Our first order of business will be setting an agenda for the competition to be held at Aquinas College in Grand Rapids."

Dr. Phelps interrupted. "Dr. Chandler, I may be out of order, but I would like to discuss a violation of ethics that recently came to my attention. It involves Dr. Reid of Alma College."

"Certainly. That will be addressed under New Business."

"Thank you."

"Unfortunately, Dr. Ruegsegger of Kalamazoo College is not able to be with us today," Dr. Chandler said. "She has submitted the report which I have distributed to you. I think we can finalize our plans for our annual debate competition based on Julie's recommendations."

"She seems to have things well-organized," Dr. Voelker offered, looking over the report.

Dr. Chandler nodded. "I think you'll agree that the main topic of conversation today should be the selection of judges and initial pairings for the competition." All heads nodded.

Dr. Chandler's secretary opened the door and stepped inside. "Pardon me for interrupting, Dr. Chandler, but I just received a phone call. I realize all of you know Dr. Reid died in a balloon accident last Saturday, but you will want to know the police have determined that she was murdered." There was a collective gasp with accompanying expressions of shock, except for Dr. Phelps who actually smiled.

"Did the caller give any more information?" Dr. Christian asked.

"No. It was Dr. Reid's secretary making several calls to colleagues, informing them before they learn of it in newspapers and television."

"I see. Thank you for telling us." The secretary retreated from the office.

Dr. Molyneux noticed Dr. Phelp's odd expression. "A smile, Margot? Why on earth would you consider this humorous?"

"All my life I have been one who sobs at good news, smiles at bad news. My body language is always the opposite of what might be considered normal, causing me acute embarrassment and humiliation. Of course, I am shocked, as are all of you, but unfortunately, my reaction gives you the impression of joy when nothing could be further from the truth."

Tuesday evening, the eleven Chemistry 231 students met at Fran Henne's parents' home in Alma. Refreshments were placed on various surfaces around the room. Students sat on chairs and the couch, or on the floor. The student leader was Bert Dugan, a sophomore in the pre-med program. He was tall and lean, as befitted the captain of Alma's MIAA champion cross-country team, and his shaved head seemed to shine like a beacon atop a lighthouse.

"Thanks for coming," Bert began. "As I said in class, I think we need a plan whereby we agree on a story so that we're consistent in police interviews."

"Why do we need to make up a story when, at least as far as I know, nobody in class killed her?" Sherry Parker asked.

"We need a story so it's obvious that we couldn't have killed her, even though we didn't," Bert replied

"It still makes no sense, Bert," Sherry replied, shaking her head.

"Remember those lacrosse players at Duke? They were accused and had their lives shaken up big-time. We don't need that."

"But they didn't make up a story," Sherry said. "They told the truth."

"Yes, and look what happened to them. If we can develop perfect alibis, we won't even be suspect, and we'll be spared the pain they endured."

"So, what's our story going to be?" Ted Skinner asked.

"It has to be simple," Sherry added.

"It's critical that any alibi proves that we weren't around either the fire or the balloon festival. If we weren't there, we aren't suspect."

"OK, so where were we?" Dick Tift asked. "We can't all be in a group somewhere — that's not logical."

"I think we should split off in groups of two or three and make up our own stories," Dick offered.

"Great suggestion, Dick! We don't need one alibi — we need four or five stories that take us out of the picture," Bert said. "Let's get into groups and create our alibis. Then we'll share plans."

"I want to go solo," Don Collins said. "I'm not good friends with anyone here."

"That's fine. Everybody else get together, in no more than threes."

For the next twenty minutes, the small groups created alibis, while Don sat apart, thinking. Then they turned back to Bert.

"Don, why don't you go first?" Bert suggested.

"Well, after Dr. Reid announced our grades, I went back to my room, gathered some things, and drove home to Port Huron. My parents were gone for the weekend, so I spent the time thinking about transferring."

"OK, great. Ted, what's your plan?"

"Sherry and I went to Dr. Reid's office and signed up to meet with her. Someone might have noticed our names on the appointment list taped to her office door. But, during the fire, and when the balloon launched, the two of us were in Mt. Pleasant, visiting some students from our hometown. We weren't, but this is our story."

"Can anyone vouch for you?" Bert asked.

"I can get someone on my dorm floor to say we went to CMU," Sherry replied.

"Okay, good. Fran, what's your story?"

"I don't think anyone will believe us, but we're going with this: We'll say we were in the library, working on term papers."

"No one can vouch for that!" Dirk Waltz scoffed, while the others chuckled. "Besides, if they review the security videos, you won't be seen on them, either coming or going. Better come up with something else!"

"Al Nowak, you're next. What's your alibi?" Bert asked.

"We were playing golf when the balloon festival was underway, and we were in the gym playing basketball when the fire started."

"Wait — don't you have to sign in to play golf?" Bert asked.

"Yeah, but I'll get my friend Will to vouch for us. He plays all the time, so I'm sure his name is on the sign-in sheet."

"And basketball — can anyone vouch for you being there at two in the morning?" Bert asked.

"I'll take care of it. I'll find someone who can tell people we were there."

"Okay, one more group. Anne Heron, what's your alibi?" Bert asked.

"We'll have two stories. Patty was at work both times, so her co-workers can truthfully vouch for her. I'll say I was visiting a high school friend who goes to Michigan State. She'll go along with it — we've been getting each other out of jams with white lies for years. This will be a piece of cake for her."

"Okay," Bert said, and, "I'm with Julie and our story is that we were doing our on-campus jobs. Julie's in maintenance, so her location can be verified. During the balloon festival, we'll say we went to the football game at U of M. My dad goes to every game, and I can get his ticket stubs — he keeps them for decades. So, we're covered."

Fran Henne spoke up, "I don't like this lying! This started out as one story, and now we have five. If the police figure out one is a lie, we'll all be doubted. I just don't like it. Since I don't think any of us did this, by lying all of us are practically admitting it."

""Fran, relax. Trust me," Bert replied. "All we need to do is give the police our alibis. Each one can be verified, so they'll have no reason to suspect any of us. And, our lives go on. The fire destroyed the exams and any grades. The balloon murderer removed Reid as an obstacle to our future careers. This is fail-safe."

"Wrong — as soon as someone says something is fail-safe, it isn't," Fran answered.

"You're making this into a big deal," Bert said sternly. "If we're interviewed, we'd simply say we weren't at Dow when the fire was started, nor were we at the balloon festival. They check it out by talking to our 'witnesses,' and bingo! — our lives go on."

"Let me ask one question. Did anyone in this room kill Dr. Reid?" Fran asked. No one responded or made a sound.

As the students fabricated alibis, Janet Reid's chase crew was together, also. The three lived in the mid-Michigan area, so they met in Ionia, intending to form a vigilante group, for they were convinced that the murderer was a rival balloonist.

Competition between Janet Reid and ballooning rival Doug Wilson had been intense, often bordering on lunacy. Both enjoyed competition and liked to improve their skills. Janet and Doug competed not only for championship ballooning titles, but for a lot of money. Janet was aware her addiction to gambling was unhealthy, and intellectually, she knew it was criminal, but the compulsion to win and to prove herself the best overrode her common sense.

Linda Ross had been Janet's crew chief for six years. Her rivalry with Sam Smith, the leader of Doug Wilson's chase crew was intense, but it didn't approach the Janet/Doug rivalry.

"Doug murdered Janet," Linda said emphatically. "This one is going to be easy for the cops to solve. It has envy and jealousy written all over it."

"Yeah, with Janet winning the last three major competitions, and Doug losing thousands of dollars on bets, it seems obvious." Barry responded, "No, Janet, nobody to pay, and no more competition for ballooning titles."

"Put the cuffs on Doug, and get to trial!" Pat True added.

"I had Janet in sight in my binoculars when she went down," Barry said. "Wilson was closest to her when it happened. When she blew up it looked like he raised his fist into the air in a victory salute."

"I heard Doug call his chase crew and say that Janet had gone down in the explosion," Pat offered. "He told them to forget about him and get to the scene to see if they could help."

"What else would you expect?" Pat asked. "He has to show he took action to help. It's called covering your tracks,"

"If the cops don't charge him, I have to act," Linda said. "Janet would expect it."

"Meaning?" Barry asked.

"Meaning, avenge her death."

"Not a good idea, Linda," Pat cautioned.

"We're a team, and teammates look after one another," Linda replied.

"Yeah, that's cool, but you had better be pretty sure he is guilty before you take any action," Barry advised. "If you're wrong — or even if you're right — you're in for a lot of trouble, maybe giving up the rest of your life."

"Yeah, let it go for awhile, and watch what develops," Pat suggested. "We'll help you, but you've got to get revenge off your mind. Understand?"

"I know you're right, but I feel like I need to support Janet somehow," Linda said.

"Janet's dead, Linda," Barry said.

"Right, and I know who did it. And I need to see that her killer feels pain!" Linda replied emotionally.

"Promise us you'll not act without our help," Pat pleaded. "Will you do that?"

"I guess so, but it won't be easy. Thanks."

SEVEN

Alma College

Lou, Jack, and Detective Jaggers conferred by phone, setting up protocols for conducting their investigation. Since Detective Jaggers had other crimes to attend to, Lou and Jack agreed to do most of the grunt work on the Reid case. Deputy Jaggers would be liaison to the sheriff, and to the prosecutor or judge if Lou and Jack needed any legal measures, like special procedures or search warrants. This arrangement left the investigating to Lou and Jack, which would help with consistency of information.

Lou and Jack arranged through Dean Atkins to meet with the students in Dr. Reid's chemistry class as a group; they also wanted to talk with each individually. They would also interview any faculty member the dean thought could offer insight into the murder.

The students would meet as a group in the dean's conference room, and the individual interviews would be held in the dean's office. Each student was informed he or she might have an attorney present if they or their parents wished. They were also told that talking to Lou and Jack was optional, but comments made in the group or individually would be submitted as evidence if relevant.

All eleven of the students consented to meet. Four students wanted family attorneys to be present. Dean Atkins would oversee the meeting.

"Thank you for coming. Mr. Searing and Mr. Kelly are on campus to investigate the murder of Dr. Reid. You are initially suspect, and I'm sure you can understand why. Dr. Reid gave most of you failing grades just before her murder. We hope that you will cooperate. Mr. Searing will begin."

"Thank you, Dean Atkins. Mr. Kelly and I also thank you for coming today. We need as much background information on Dr. Reid as we can get as we work on solving her murder. We hope you can help us understand this woman. You may offer comments, or you may remain silent. In addition to this group meeting, we may want to talk privately with some, if not all, of you."

Ken Renaud, the attorney representing Ted Skinner spoke up. "Are any electronic devices operating in this room?"

"No," Lou replied. "We'll take notes, but there is no recording."

"Thank you," the attorney said. "While I'm here to represent Ted Skinner, I would like to caution all the students to think before speaking."

"That's fair," Lou said. "We're not here because we suspect any of you are involved. One or more of you could be, but at the moment we have no reason to suspect anyone in particular. We simply want to know about Dr. Reid. On the other hand, if any of you know something about this crime we hope you would share that, either in this group or in person later. So, under these ground rules, would anyone like to speak?" Lou asked.

After a pause long enough for Lou and Jack to wonder if anyone would talk, Bert Dugan spoke up.

"Perhaps I can't speak for everyone, but I thank you for coming and talking to us. All of us want this solved. Murder is a sin, and evil is wrong and disturbing in a peaceful society, especially on this campus where Jesus Christ serves as a model for living. So, thank you."

"You're welcome," Lou responded.

Bert continued. "Then I want to point out that most of us are at Alma to get a good undergraduate education. Many of us want to go on to graduate school. We're aware that competition to get into the best schools is fierce. A high grade-point average is critical to our future. We're under a lot of stress, because we know we must excel here at Alma to have any chance of being accepted into post-graduate programs.

"Dr. Reid decked us with an impossible exam, asking questions that had no relevance to material we had studied," Bert continued. "Most of us received failing grades, which would go on our transcripts, and that would get us off to a terrible start. That was simply unfair, and we're the victims in that sense.

"Regardless, we are Christians, raised in Christian homes, active in Christian churches at home and here on campus. We value life, and we take the Commandments seriously. So I would be shocked if anyone in this class was involved in the professor's murder. I wanted to set the stage for you, so to speak."

"Thank you," Lou replied. "I attended Alma, and Jack went to Aquinas, so we understand stress and high academic standards, don't we, Jack?" Jack nodded. "Anyone else?"

Anne Heron spoke up. "I'll tell you something about this woman: she loved her subject, but not the people in her classes. She seemed to enjoy watching her students suffer. She probably thought she was toughening us up, but in reality she was creating unreasonable frustration for us. She gave exams over material that was totally foreign to us. She favored athletes. Whatever the psychological term is for people who like to inflict pain, she was it. This sounds sick, but I'd almost like to hug whoever killed her, because the school and the students can breathe easier for no longer feeling bullied."

Lou turned toward the Dean. "Dean Atkins, are you hearing this for the first time?" Lou asked.

Dean Atkins sighed. "There have been complaints. Our president has emphasized tougher academic standards at Alma, and we expect the faculty to make students work hard for good grades. But, there was no expectation of making students suffer or of treating them unfairly. Dr. Reid explained to me that some of her test material assumed knowledge from previous classes, and while a student might say she tested what she hadn't presented, the material should be understood by any sophomore chemistry student. Yes, I heard complaints from students, and from a few parents. I talked to Professor Reid and at the time I felt she understood my concerns, but obviously she did not change her behavior."

"Can someone tell us about Dr. Reid's last class?" Lou asked. After about thirty seconds, Fran Henne spoke up.

"She walked into the classroom and returned our exams from her briefcase. Then she gave us a lecture about how all of us were high achievers in our home towns, and how we were the leaders of the future. She said our poor showing on the exam would hurt our GPAs and interfere with our getting into graduate schools."

"And how did your classmates handle this?" Lou asked.

"In a variety of ways. My guess is that each of us did whatever was a stress-reliever for us. Some probably shoved fists into pillows, and I imagine some prayed."

"Did anyone storm out of the class?" Jack asked. "Did anyone threaten Dr. Reid in front of the others?"

"The class only met for the return of exams and answering questions," Fran Henne said. "We didn't storm out of the room, and I don't recall anyone threatening her to her face. But the words used outside would probably embarrass us and the college if they were made public."

Jack spoke up. "Forgive my pointing a finger, but a logical reaction to perceived abuse is to attack. In psychological theory, punishment leads to either escape or aggression. You couldn't escape the reality of what just happened, so it seems that aggression would follow. I wouldn't expect anyone to admit in front of this group to being involved in killing Dr. Reid. But, you need to know that you all are suspect, although innocent until proven guilty."

Attorney Joe Grover stood. "It appears to me that you and Mr. Searing came here believing that the murderer is in this class. Is that what you're implying?"

"Absolutely not!" Lou responded sharply. "Mr. Kelly is simply being honest. It's logical to suspect a spouse when someone is murdered. In this case, the victim's family appears to have been her students. It's logical to ask because crimes of passion are nearly always committed by someone who feels wronged, and revenge is a very strong emotion. Mr. Kelly is simply saying you are automatically suspect, individually, and as a group. Once we talk with you, I expect we'll confirm your non-involvement. But Jack and I do not sugar-coat anything. You'll hear the truth from us, just as we expect the truth from you."

"We understand, but don't you see that you are acting like Dr. Reid — frightening these young people?" attorney Grover continued. "You're telling them they probably did it, and that will be your theory until they can prove they didn't do it. Shame on you, Mr. Searing!"

Dean Atkins intervened. "Mr. Searing and Mr. Kelly have a tough job to do after a terrible tragedy. They have the students' best interests at heart, and their honesty, quite frankly, is refreshing."

Bert Dugan rose. "We welcome the questions you'll ask us individually. We're stressed about a lot of things right now. We're reeling from failing grades, which we think — no, we know — were unfair, and now we find we're suspects in our professor's death. I don't think the attorney's comment represents our thinking. We're ready and willing to explain our activities following Dr. Reid's death. The sooner her murder is solved, the better."

"Thank you. Jack and I appreciate your comments. Now we'll interview some of you in person. We'll be asking you where you were when Professor Reid's office was burned, and, where you were the next morning when the murder occurred. If people can verify your stories, give us their names. OK? We know everyone would prefer to be first, but someone has to be last, so we ask your patience."

Suddenly, Suzanne Starmann rose from her chair and pounded the table with her fists. "I can save all of these people time and trouble. I killed Professor Reid. I burned her office. I alone am responsible for both acts." Suzanne calmed herself, and tears ran down her cheeks. "Let my friends go so they can get on with their lives. I'm not a threat to anyone. I don't have a weapon. I'll go to the police station voluntarily. And, I want to say, I am so sorry." Sharon came over to comfort her. Suzanne shook her head. "I feel so guilty. I never should have done it."

Dean Atkins stepped outside the conference room and called campus security on his cell phone. No one panicked, but the students were directed to leave the room. Jack took Suzanne by the arm and brought her around the table to Lou. Lou asked the attorneys present, "Does one of you represent this young woman?" They shook their heads. "Then I ask that one of you remain with the three of us until the authorities get here, to see that her rights are not violated." Attorney Renaud offered his services.

Campus police had jurisdiction, but they called the city police, who gave authority to Lou as had been agreed upon with Sheriff Pritchard. Lou suggested Suzanne be taken to a quiet office and offered some water. The dean asked Becca Norris, Director of the Development Office to be with Suzanne and attorney Renaud while Lou talked with a few people.

Jack got to work immediately with an Alma officer and a detective from the Gratiot County Sheriff's Department. The student was identified as Suzanne Starmann from Grand Ledge. Within minutes

Jack reached Mrs. Starmann by phone. The news was disturbing, but Mrs. Starmann was sure the confession was related to Suzanne's mental health. Terri Starmann explained that Suzanne was undergoing therapy for an Obsessive Compulsive Disorder (OCD). She would ask her daughter's psychiatrist to call and explain. She told Jack that on one other occasion Suzanne had seen a car accident and told the police she was responsible. Or if a violent crime occurred, Suzanne was certain it was her fault. Medications had helped, Terri Starmann explained, but her daughter admitting to setting a fire on campus and murdering a professor was not beyond the realm of possibility for her.

When Lou entered the room, Suzanne was crying but otherwise calm. "How are you doing?" Lou began, showing compassion for the coed.

"I'm so sorry. I really am."

"Please tell me your name."

"Suzanne Starmann."

"Suzanne, please try to relax and tell me what happened. Okay?"

"I set the fire, and I killed Dr. Reid."

"Let's take these one at a time. How did you set the fire?" Lou asked. Before Suzanne could answer, there was a knock on the door. Lou rose and opened it, stepped outside briefly while Jack told Lou of Mrs. Starmann's comments. Lou thanked Jack and reentered the room.

Lou apologized. "I'm sorry, Suzanne. Now, you were going to explain how you started the fire."

"I wanted to destroy grades and any evidence of the failed exams. I thought a fire was the best way to do this."

"So, how did you carry this out?" Lou asked, looking straight into her eyes.

Suzanne refused to meet his gaze. "I went into the building late at night," Suzanne began. "Dr. Reid's office door was locked, but I had a small container of gasoline. I poured it out and let it seep under the door. I dropped a lighted match onto it and quickly got out of the building."

"What time was this?"

"I'd say one in the morning."

"I would think the building was locked at night," Lou remarked.

"Normally it is," Suzanne explained. "A security guard makes rounds around ten. I know the guard, and I asked him to leave the building open, saying I had to take a paper to a professor's office, and I wouldn't be finished till after midnight. He agreed to leave the east door unlocked. That's another reason for my confession. I figured he would tell the police about me, and I'd be a very logical suspect."

"It appears you succeeded in destroying the exam records."

"I hope I did. I just couldn't allow anyone to know about the exam, the grades, or any correspondence with parents or the Registrar."

"Now, about the murder of Dr. Reid?" Lou said.

Suzanne sighed. "What do you want to know?"

"Let's begin with this; did you act alone or with others?"

"Alone."

"How did you kill Dr. Reid?"

"It is quite complicated."

"Complicated?" Lou replied. "As I understand it, you got word of the failed exam at around nine-thirty Friday morning, October 1, and she was killed the next morning in Battle Creek. Do you mean you were planning this even before the exam grades were announced?"

"Oh, no. After I found out about the grades and saw how my friends were hurt, I went on the Internet, my second reason for confessing, because you guys would take my computer and discover this anyway. I learned that the best way to kill someone in a hot air balloon is to put a small bomb next to one of the tanks in the wicker basket."

"And where did you get this bomb?" Lou asked.

"The Internet site tells you how to make it. I stole everything I needed from our science labs."

"Suzanne, do you have any health problems that might explain your behavior?"

"No. I don't think so. I'm sure I did this. I'm so sorry. I feel so guilty."

"Are you seeing a psychiatrist now?"

"Dr. Daugherty. I'm counseling with him."

"I see. Would it be okay with you if I talked with him?"

"I guess so."

"Do you have his phone number with you?" Lou asked.

Suzanne did; she gave it to Lou, who dialed the physician on his cell phone.

"This is Lou Searing calling," he told the receptionist. "I have a situation at Alma College involving a patient of Dr. Daugherty and I need to speak with him."

"The patient's name please."

"Suzanne Starmann."

Lou listened, then said, "I'll wait, thank you."

Suzanne spoke softly as he waited. "I don't have a criminal mind. That woman was evil. Somebody had to save the lives of my friends. I saw that the administration wouldn't do anything. If I could kill Dr. Reid, I could save my friends' lives. I was willing to sacrifice that so they could continue their educations."

"I understand," Lou replied, waiting for the doctor to pick up the phone.

"Hello, this is Dr. Daugherty. Is this Mr. Searing?"

"Yes, thank you for taking my call." Lou excused himself and went out of the room. "I am at Alma College with Suzanne Starmann, who has given me permission to talk with you. She has confessed to two major crimes — arson and murder. My associate, Jack Kelly, has talked with her mother who indicates that Suzanne has a mental heath disorder. Can you explain this?"

"I have diagnosed Suzanne as having Obsessive Compulsive Disorder."

"Meaning?"

"Meaning, she often believes that she's experiencing something, or in this case, is responsible for something which she has not experienced, and for which she is not responsible."

"Like admitting she set fire to a professor's office?"

"Yes, that is a good example. People with this disorder often believe they did something and feel guilty about it, when in reality they had nothing to do with the event they imagine. I am sure she didn't commit the murder either. My guess is that she is showing great remorse, is apologizing for what happened, is repeatedly saying she is sorry."

"Yes, that is what is happening," Lou replied. "I'm curious, how can she cope in a demanding program like Alma with such a condition?"

"She was auditing sophomore chemistry, not seeking credit or a grade. We are examining her to see if she is mentally fit to re enter college and withstand the pressures of academia. She was a terrific chemistry student in high school. She and her parents hope she can get an advanced degree in forensic science."

"I see. But is there still the possibility that Suzanne really committed these crimes and is hiding behind her health problem?"

"I suppose so, but I am ninety-nine percent sure she didn't."

"But that still leaves a chance, doesn't it?" Lou asked. "Thanks for your help, Doctor. I appreciate your taking time to help me understand Suzanne's medical condition."

While outside the room, Lou talked with Jack and Chief of Police Worthington. "We don't have enough for an arrest. The medical condition is clear, and I personally doubt she could make a bomb. My guess is when Jack asks campus security if they left a door open last night they will say, 'Of course not.' I suggest we release her, keeping the possibility that she committed one or both crimes in our minds. I don't think she should be left alone on campus. News has already spread about her confession, and she couldn't handle wading through the sea of public opinion, comments, and media attention. Jack, please call her mother to come and get her, and in the meantime, find a roommate or friend who can be with her, collect her belongings and protect her from speaking to anyone, especially the media."

Lou returned to the room. "Shall we continue, Suzanne?"

"I'm not looking to be a martyr or anything," Suzanne began. "I saw a terrible injustice, and I acted. Most people see my action as unconscionable, but I consider it heroic. Life goes on."

"Suzanne, we're not going to arrest you for these crimes," Lou said. "You're free to go, and your mother will be coming to take you home. Someone will stay with you till your mom gets here. You should return to the dorm and collect whatever you want to take with you. Dr. Daugherty will most likely see you soon. Thanks for talking with me."

"I'm so sorry."

"I know you are, Suzanne."

Dean Atkins and President Shanks were relieved that the campus was relatively quiet when Suzanne confessed. Anyone curious about the emergency vehicles probably thought that someone in the administration building had a medical problem, a stroke or heart attack or fainting. However, as students who had witnessed the encounter went back to classes, word of Suzanne's confession spread across campus like a wildfire on a dry prairie. Lou and Jack decided not to conduct individual interviews then, reserving the privilege for later.

EIGHT

Following Suzanne's questioning, Lou and Jack arranged to meet Reid's chase crew at Champps restaurant in Lansing's Eastwood Mall. The group of three people in the sports bar seemed to recognize them and waved half-heartedly, so Lou and Jack approached, greeted all, and sat down, taking a moment to relax.

After introductions of all present, and ordering a Diet Coke with lime, Lou began. "How is everyone doing? You've been through quite an ordeal, probably feeling fear, disgust, and anger."

"I think we're doing okay," Linda replied, looking at her friends. "Every hour or so we seem to think about Janet, and the nightmare of seeing that basket explode comes to mind. That was horrific."

"Yes, I'm sure it was, but our investigation needs to include your observations," Lou said. "So, to obtain justice for Janet, I'm going to ask some pointed questions, whose answers may help us solve this crime against your friend." The three nodded in understanding.

"Who could have murdered Janet?" Lou asked.

Linda spoke first. "My initial thought was that the murderer was someone with Doug Wilson's crew. Doug and Janet were very competitive — and jealous of each other. They were not friends. In fact, Janet told me that if anything ever happened to her or her balloon, to suspect Doug and his team first. So when the balloon exploded, there was no question in my mind that they caused it."

"Do you still believe this?" Lou asked.

"Yeah, I do," Linda answered. "As I said, there was a lot of jealousy, and most people don't know that a lot of money rides on events, with payments under the table, or not at all. Janet maintained that Doug didn't pay his debts, and she had been quite upset about that lately."

"Could anyone else have done this?" Jack asked.

Barry spoke up. "A lot of attention has been focused on Janet's chemistry students, but I don't think they're suspects. None of them was involved in ballooning, and to kill Janet in thin air took a good knowledge of the sport. I understand their anger, and I might be first to point the finger toward them, but ballooning technology is too specialized for someone not involved in the sport."

"The most obvious suspect to me — and I assume to you at this point — is the balloonmeister," Pat added.

"What's a balloonmeister?" Lou asked.

"The balloonmeister is the overseer of the balloon events," Barry replied.

"Like an umpire or referee?" Lou asked.

"Yeah, I guess so. He decides whether the balloons go up, given wind speed. He determines who gets into the lift area. He decides if the balloons are safe to fly. He determines which events are going to be held. He's in total charge."

"Thanks, Pat, you were saying," Lou said, looking to Pat.

"Eric Swanson was the balloonmeister at the Battle Creek festival. He's the best, actually. Anyway, he inspected each balloon and he knows ballooning. Eric was angry with Janet because she dropped him from a book contract. A lot of things point to him, Mr. Searing. You have a motive, revenge; you have a weapon, a small bomb. And, Eric Swanson was at the site where the murder was set up, which was at the festival as the balloons were being prepped."

"Sounds convincing," Lou concluded. The three nodded.

"Did you notice anyone near your space in the lift area who shouldn't have been there?"

"No," Barry replied immediately. "All of us are observant. We had specific jobs to do, but we felt responsible for that balloon. In fact, it was my responsibility to see that the basket was safe and ready for inspection by the balloonmeister. There was no bomb in the basket when I checked it, either attached to the propane tanks or anywhere near the tanks. The only person who came near us and the balloon that morning was Eric Swanson."

"It sounds like you're convinced that Eric Swanson murdered Dr. Reid," Lou summarized.

"Yes, but we only decided that recently, Lou. At first, we were sure the murderer was someone in Doug's crew. But after the anger faded, Barry and I decided it had to be Eric, for the reasons Pat mentioned."

"In spite of the explosion, evidence technicians were able to lift a good print off a piece of the bomb casing," Lou said. "They can't match the print, so it must belong to someone not on the criminal print registry. This doesn't mean it isn't Mr. Swanson's print — it simply means the killer hasn't committed a previous felony." The three frowned, shaking their heads.

"Have you looked into the possibility that someone fired a rifle into the basket, hitting the propane tank?" Pat asked.

"As far as I know, no one has suggested that," Jack replied.

"Well, I think you should check that out," Pat continued. "If a bullet punctured a tank, it would mean the murderer was someone outside the lift area at the event."

"I disagree with Barry and Pat, I believe Doug Wilson is responsible for Janet's death," Linda said, with conviction. "Either he did it, or he paid someone to do it. I'll go to my grave believing that."

"So, you've identified two suspects, Eric and Doug," Jack summarized.

"We thank you for meeting with us," Lou said, before once again expressing his sympathy for the loss of their friend.

Lou and Jack arrived in Portland late in the afternoon on their way home from questioning the students and Janet's chase crew. Over coffee and a piece of pie at Betty's Café, Jack got serious for a moment. "What do you think of Suzanne's confession?"

"She didn't do it, Jack. I'm confused about the OCD and the potential for a real crime. My gut reaction is that she pulled that off so that there wouldn't be any individual interviews."

"How do you know that?"

"Should a magician have to give away all of his secrets?" Lou asked.

"Seriously, how can you believe that?" Jack asked, eager to learn.

"Well, in the first place, I showed you the fire marshal's report. He says the fire was an accident."

"I know, but he could be wrong, you know," Jack replied.

"That's true, but my money is on the fire marshal. And, secondly, Suzanne's psychiatrist believes strongly that she acted as she did because of her mental health. And third, Suzanne is a drama major. She wasn't registered in Dr. Reid's class, she had no conflict with Dr. Reid, and she'll not return to Alma College."

"You knew this going into the meeting?" Jack asked.

"Jack, working on a case is a lot like becoming a salesman. Before you meet a client, you find out as much as you can about him or, in this case, her. You learn how best to deal with her."

"What else did you know?"

"I knew she was going to do what she did."

"No way!" Jack exclaimed. "How could you know?"

"Ok, I didn't know exactly what she'd do, but I knew she'd do something. As the students came in, I spent the time watching people, as did you. I noticed that the class leader — the one who said he disagreed with the attorney — was talking with her as if they were planning something. He appeared to be giving her instructions, and as she demonstrated, I think I was right. So, I can't be certain, but I'm fairly sure the confession was staged, and we'll eventually discover that she had nothing to do with either the fire or the murder."

"So, the bigger issue is whether the class did have something to do with the fire and murder," Jack said, finally catching on to what was happening.

"I think so. Now we conduct some individual interviews and go from there."

"She should be getting good grades in drama — she fooled me," Jack remarked ruefully.

"Live and learn. Now let's go home to Carol and Elaine." Lou paid for the pie and coffee and left a good tip which he often did when he felt it was deserved.

As the two men passed the Lowell Exit on I-96 Lou's cell phone rang. He answered and listened briefly. "Thanks for calling, Sheriff. I figured you'd want to know how the interview with the student confessor went, so I was going to call you. Jack and I are driving home, so I'll put my phone on speaker so Jack can hear."

"Not a problem." The Sheriff's voice came through clearly.

"It's all so sad, Sheriff. According to her psychiatrist, Suzanne Starmann has OCD and simply thought she was guilty. She explained what she did and why she did it, but what she offered contradicts the fire marshal's report, and we're quite certain she didn't make a bomb from material in the science labs. But, we are not simply checking her off; she might be feigning the psychosis to commit crimes, but at this point, we can't wrap up this case."

"I understand. We have some OCD folks who stop at accident scenes and tell us they are sure they are at fault, when in fact they had nothing to do with the accident."

"There was no arrest. Suzanne's mother is on her way to Alma to take her home, to get her away from the stares and comments."

"Thanks for the update, Lou."

"Certainly. We'll stay in touch, Sheriff."

When Linda Ross, of Janet Reid's chase crew, heard of the student's confession she set up a conference call with Barry and Pat to discuss it.

"Boloney! They're dealing with a wacko! That student had nothing to do with Janet's murder," Linda said to her friends.

"You think Doug Wilson is setting up the game to shift attention from him onto students at Alma?" Barry asked.

"That would be my guess."

"Are you going to tell the police what you're thinking?" Pat asked.

"No. I'm just going to kill Doug and avenge Janet's murder. Janet would want me to act. Wouldn't you agree?"

"I guess so," Pat replied. "Janet sure had little love for Doug."

"Why wait for an investigation, trial, and all that boloney?" Linda asked. "Doug killed Janet — we know it. So let's just kill Wilson, and then we can close the book."

"You know it, Linda," Pat stated firmly. "I think Eric Swanson is behind this, not Doug."

"I just don't want to go to jail for the rest of my life," Barry said.

"You're not going to jail, and neither am I," said Linda confidently.

"It can't take too many grey cells to find a foolproof way of killing a guy," Barry replied.

"How are you going to do it, Linda?" Pat asked.

"I guess I'll go to the Internet and see what I can find."

"Are you crazy? Haven't you heard of people who do that? They kill someone, their computer is confiscated, and bingo! Crime solved!" Barry said.

"Yes, but that's if the police have a suspect," Linda replied.

"We won't be suspects?" Pat said. "We're friends of the woman who was Wilson's fiercest competitor. I can't think of a more logical murderer for Doug Wilson than those grieving Janet Reid's loss who would logically think her competitor did it."

"Ok, ok, I won't go on the Internet," Linda replied. "It will be easy enough anyway."

"No, it won't, Linda. Not these days," Barry predicted. "There are a lot more ways to investigate murder and to prove a suspect's involvement. Let's hold off on this, okay?"

"I'm doing this with a well-thought-out plan," Linda said. "Are you with me or not?"

"I don't think we can pull it off, and besides, I have other plans for my life than spending it in some women's penitentiary," Pat True admitted.

"Ok, but if the cops ever suspect me, I'll believe you tipped them off," Linda was angry. "And you don't want to upset me, Pat. Am I clear?"

"You needn't worry about me. I may be a coward but I'm not stupid. Upsetting you is the last thing I would ever do, Linda."

"Good!" Linda replied. "Now find a good alibi, because we never had this conversation, nor did we meet."

"No, we didn't meet today, and we never talked about Doug Wilson as Janet's murderer," Pat said, her voice rising with emotion. "Our lips are sealed. I'm getting off the call. Good luck to you, and I'll be praying that you come to your senses."

NINE

Lou always made a point of attending a victim's funeral. He was curious about who attended, who sat with whom, who cried, who said what, who came to the reception, who left early. Sometimes the biggest clues concerned who was not there. To be effective, Lou needed to know what to look for before attending, which was sometimes difficult to manage, because services are often held soon after a murder. At Janet's funeral there was no family, so Lou lacked a major resource for who Reid had been, her relationships, and who might be expected to attend but didn't.

Lou understood that Professor Dykstra of the philosophy department had stepped in to handle arrangements and make decisions for the college. Through the professor, Lou learned who would be at the funeral, and Dr. Dykstra would sit with Lou behind the mourners to answer questions if they arose. Lou could observe the mourners and Dr. Dykstra could slip out to attend to last-minute details.

Dr. Dykstra didn't expect any students to attend. Dr. Reid was not liked by her students and not particularly respected by the faculty. In fact, Dr. Dykstra predicted that those taking time to attend the funeral would be people sharing her passion for ballooning.

Lou noticed that the charity for memorial donations was neither Alma College nor a ballooning association, but Gamblers Anonymous. Dr. Dykstra explained that Dr. Reid's mother, who had chosen not to attend the funeral because she and her daughter had been estranged for many years, had requested that designation.

The funeral was held in the Dunning Memorial Chapel on the Alma campus and attended by only about twenty people. Dr. Dykstra noted that the college contingent were probably there out of a societal commitment and a sense of duty. Those from the ballooning community were few because to attend required traveling some distance to a place not reachable by commercial airlines. Also, the service schedule coincided with a ballooning event in southern Indiana.

"Who is that young man on the far side by the front?" Lou asked Dr. Dykstra in a whisper.

"That's Al Nowak, a student."

"Nice of him to come," Lou said. "He must have some respect for the professor."

"I can't say," Dykstra remarked. "But he's a good kid."

"He was in Janet Reid's chemistry class. And who are the three people on our side down by the front?" Lou asked.

"I don't know, but they are not Alma people. The woman two rows in front of us is President Shanks, of course; her husband Gerald is on her right."

"May I have a copy of the guest book in the lobby?" Lou asked.

"Yes, I can do that."

"Thanks. I appreciate your help today."

"You're welcome. I hope you can get to the bottom of this," Dr. Dykstra said. "The woman wasn't popular, but her death is upsetting, and the college community won't be comfortable until it is explained."

Following the funeral, Lou got a call from Detective Jaggers. "I'm on my way to do a second search of Janet Reid's home office. Would you like to join me?"

"Most definitely. Where is her home and when do I need to be there?"

"I have the warrant so we can do the search any time, but the sooner the better."

"The funeral and reception are over, so I can come right away," Lou replied.

"That's fine. Her apartment is 555 Wright Avenue, Number seven."

"I'll be there. What convinced the judge to issue another warrant?" Lou asked, realizing the sheriff had gotten an initial warrant soon after the murder.

"All I heard about was the grading sheet, but I have a hunch that something else is behind this mess. Maybe her past mail will offer a clue. Something internal to the college might be helpful."

"I agree. Okay, I'll head over and see you in a few minutes."

Detective Jaggers had waited in his vehicle for Lou to pull up. Once the men greeted one another, they entered the apartment and began looking around. Everything in Janet's apartment was neat and well-organized. The focus of this search was the home office, but the detectives quickly scanned the rest of the apartment looking for anything that might arouse their curiosity. They found nothing unusual.

Janet's computer, taken from the apartment under the previous order, had yielded nothing of interest. It was filled with scientific papers, research data, personal correspondence, ballooning websites, and numerous syllabi for chemistry courses.

Lou decided to tackle the four-drawer file cabinet, while the deputy looked through the desk, an antique roll-top with many small compartments and numerous drawers. The tedious work unearthed nothing of interest until Lou lifted an overstuffed folder out of the second drawer from the top. "This may be something."

"What do you have?" Bob asked.

"Looks like a manuscript. This thing is huge."

"Something about chemistry?" Bob asked.

"No, ballooning. A book apparently: The History of Ballooning in America: A Compendium of Stories, Facts, Records, and Photos. Says here in the introduction, 'Never before has such an effort been undertaken. This book represents years of ballooning and has been researched and written by Janet Reid, an International Champion Pilot, and Eric Swanson, America's most experienced Balloonmeister.'"

"So, they were writing a book together. I haven't heard of this Swanson, have you?" Deputy Jaggers asked.

"His name came up yesterday in talking with Reid's chase crew," Lou offered. "Who's the publisher?"

"Some outfit out of New York — Long Island Publishing. It has a copyright of 2009."

"That's odd, isn't it?" Bob asked.

"Not really. Often, if a book is published in the fall, the publisher will have the upcoming year as the copyright year. We need to look for correspondence between Reid, Swanson, and Long Island Publishing. And I'll call them right now. Ok?"

"Fine."

Lou took out his cell phone and dialed the number he found on a piece of correspondence from the publisher.

MURDER IN THIN AIR

When a receptionist answered, Lou said, "I would like to talk to the editor for a book being published by your company. The title is The History of Ballooning in America."

"One moment please." Lou switched his phone to speaker.

"Hello. This is Pat Wellard. May I help you?"

"I hope so. This is Lou Searing calling from Michigan. I have in my hand a manuscript written by a Janet Reid and an Eric Swanson entitled, The History of Ballooning in America."

"Yes, I'm familiar with the book."

"Ms. Wellard, are you aware that Janet Reid died recently?" Lou asked.

"Oh, yes. Such a loss. We're proceeding with the book with Mr. Swanson as sole author."

"Is that legal? I mean, I'm sure your attorney would tell me it is. But it seems that Janet's estate attorney would want some say in this."

"We have consulted our attorney, as you presumed," Ms. Wellard explained. "In this case, the writing credit and royalties go to the junior author."

"Was this spelled out in a legal document?" Lou asked.

"I can't answer that, Mr. Searing," Ms. Wellard replied.

"Hmmm, a bit strange isn't it?"

"Well, this entire book has been strange, if truth be told."

"In what way?"

"First, I was informed that Reid and Swanson had a falling out, and that the book would be authored by Janet Reid," Ms. Wellard began. "Swanson looked into the legality of breaking their contract and learned that what Janet had done was, in fact, legal. But Swanson felt betrayed, stabbed in the back, more like. This book, Mr. Searing, is expected to be huge. Our marketing department projects sales in the millions."

"I didn't know the ballooning world was that big."

"Every library in America will want this book," Pat explained. "Even school libraries will want it. The photos alone will be worth the price of the book, not to mention that the scientific information goes back to the beginning of man's early attempts at flight. Many of the stories are never-before-told and are entertaining. I mean, Reid and Swanson worked for years on this."

"So, when Janet was killed, Swanson and his attorney worked with your attorney to put his name as sole author instead of Reid and Swanson?"

"Yes."

"It hardly seems fair for Swanson to get credit for the compendium when Reid did at least half the work."

"I'm the editor, not an attorney," Ms Wellard explained, "I'm careful not to get involved with matters beyond my purview."

"I understand. Well, thanks for this information."

"You're welcome. Good-bye."

Lou turned off the phone, turned to Deputy Jaggers, and said, "As you heard, one more suspect, a guy by the name of Eric Swanson."

"Okay, the more the merrier, I guess."

Lou said, "This book deal might be a motive. And Swanson was on the grounds while the balloons were being prepared for lift, correct?"

"As much on the grounds as a baseball umpire would be in Yankee Stadium," Deputy Jaggers replied, proud of his quickly conceived analogy.

The two men examined papers for the next hour, but they found nothing as interesting as the book, now with only one author.

On a hunch, Lou called Pat Wellard at Long Island Publishing again before they left. Like Lt. Columbo of 1970s TV, Lou always seemed to have one more question. He asked, "The most recent manuscript — who is noted as the author?"

"Janet Reid," Pat replied.

"And why is this? Doesn't the contract with your company show an author and co-author?"

"You'll need to contact the business office for that, Mr. Searing."

"I will. But as far as you know, the agreement was for the two of them to co-author a book, and the most recent manuscript has only one author, Janet Reid. Now, with her death, the new author is Eric Swanson. Do I have it right?"

"As the editor, yes, that is my understanding."

"Thank you, Ms.Wellard."

Lou looked into his little book of important phone numbers and called the Battle Creek Balloon Festival. "Good day, Lou Searing here. I'm investigating Janet Reid's death. Can you answer a question for me?" Lou paused and looked at Deputy Jaggers.

"Who was the balloonmeister at your event?" Lou asked. He nodded more positively. "Eric Swanson. Thank you. Do you have a phone number, address, or e-mail address for him?" Lou quickly jotted notes in his notebook.

"Thank you very much." He closed the phone. "Swanson lives in Indianapolis."

Lou decided to call Eric. He was on a roll. Swanson did not answer the phone, but Lou left a message asking him to call back.

About a half-hour later as the two were about to lock up the Reid apartment, Lou's phone rang. "Mr. Searing, this is Eric Swanson. You called earlier."

Lou put the phone on speaker. "Thanks for calling. As I mentioned in my voice message, I'm assisting the Calhoun County sheriff in investigating the death of Janet Reid."

"Terrible loss. I still can't get my mind off the tragedy."

"I understand you were the balloonmeister for the Battle Creek Festival."

"Yes I was and I feel a bit guilty about that."

"Guilty?" Lou asked, puzzled at Eric's response.

"One of my many responsibilities is to do a safety check of each entry and obviously, I missed something with Janet's equipment."

"What do you think could have caused the explosion?"

"The propane tank had to be punctured in some way. The explosion would not have occurred without a flame and fuel. You need both."

"A gas leak maybe?"

"I suppose anything is possible, but a rifle shot could have punctured the propane tank too."

"I see. Mr. Swanson, how do you inspect the envelopes, baskets, and equipment before a lift?"

"I have a list of checks, too numerous to mention over the phone. Most are visual checks, but many involve connections, attachments, or hookups. I also review the pilot's license and any recent maintenance that has been done on the envelope or anything in the basket."

"I understand that you are the one who allows people into the lift area."

"Yes, the festival staff issues credentials to those allowed inside."

"How does that work?"

"Each pilot provides the names of their crews. The festival people prepare wrist-bands that mustn't be removed for the duration of the festival. Media people have tags they must wear. And security people are obvious by their uniforms."

"Might you allow someone into the lift area who isn't credentialed?"

"I have power to do that, yes, but I seldom exercise it. There's little reason for anyone to be in the lift area who is not a pilot, a member of the crew preparing the balloon for lift, a media rep, or security."

"Have you ever had to remove unauthorized people from the lift area?"

"Yes. At every festival, someone tries to break the rules. It might be a spouse hoping to give a kiss for luck, a friend of a pilot or crew member, or sometimes a local photographer who doesn't realize — or won't admit to knowing — that a credential is necessary. Making sure that only authorized people are in the lift area and protected is my job, Mr. Searing."

"I see. You knew Janet Reid?" Lou asked.

"Oh yes. I considered her a friend."

"I understand you were co-authoring a book with her."

There was a pause. "You raise a disturbing and sensitive point."

"Sorry. Can you talk about it?" Lou inquired.

"She stabbed me in the back. We had worked together on a book for about five years. It was going to be the finest book about ballooning, bar none. Then she suddenly told me she was going it alone. She informed the publisher and editor that the book was hers."

"Disturbing and sensitive don't scratch the surface," Lou replied. "If someone did that to me, I'd just about be out of control."

"Well, I was. I met with an attorney and even sought counseling. I tried to talk to her, but she wouldn't change her mind. My attorney told me I could sue her, but that I probably wouldn't win. So, not only would I lose years of royalties, I might lose thousands in legal fees."

"Mr. Swanson, I'm sure you understand our interest in whether Janet's death might be related to this conflict. You may not be a suspect personally, but can you understand the possibility that someone representing you might want revenge for this injustice?"

"Of course. I figured sooner or later someone like you would knock on my door. I may look like I have a target on my back, but you'll discover, as obvious as that may appear, I am not the murderer of Janet Reid."

"I appreciate your cooperation, Mr. Swanson. If you think of anything else that might help, I trust you'll let me know."

"I will."

Lou drove home after the funeral and the search of Janet's apartment. It had been a long day. A walk on the shore was often a good time for Carol to get caught up on what Lou was learning in his crime-solving. Tonight they wore jackets as they walked well after dark, by light of a full moon over Lake Michigan, with a few beach bonfires to warm the cool fall air.

"How goes it with the Alma prof's murder?" Carol asked.

"It's too early to make much of it."

"No suspects?"

"Oh, the world is a stage, I suppose," Lou replied. "The victim was not popular with her students, so someone could have taken revenge for a grade or some other slight. The woman was a ballooning champion, which stirs jealousy of other balloonists. Her mother, from whom she is estranged, made Gamblers Anonymous the memorial charity, so maybe she owed a lot of money and didn't pay up."

"Or maybe somebody owed her a lot of money and found murder an easier pay-back than money," Carol wondered. "Lots of possibilities for you."

"Yeah, unfortunately. No other family in this one, unlike the last one."

"At least you'll learn all about hot air ballooning," Carol said.

"Yes, and that reminds me. Jack and I are going up in a balloon to experience it. I thought you probably would want to go. He was going to check with Elaine and..."

"Are you nuts?" Carol broke in, giving Lou a startled look. "No way!"

Lou was startled. "With a balloon, you're just floating along. After all, you like flying."

"Don't they let go of the tether?" Carol asked.

"Sure. That's how you float."

"But, how would I get back down if I needed to?" Carol inquired.

Lou was bewildered. "I don't know. Why would you need to get down?"

"Because I might not be able to handle it."

"Floating in the air?"

"I'd be up in the sky — suspended. No way, Lou! You go, and I'll watch."

"Elaine is going."

"Won't work, Lou. I don't care if the Pope is going."

"Okay, okay. I get the message."

When Lou entered his office after the walk with Carol, he found a fax in the printer tray. It was a message from Dean Atkins: "Lou, thought you might be interested to know that Dr. Reid turned in her grades before the fire. This is a copy of the grade sheet."

Lou looked over the grades. These sure aren't failing grades, he thought. The grades sent to the registrar were all As except one D, for Don Collins. Lou considered the list. They probably excelled in quizzes, term papers, class participation. If one or more of the students killed her over the mid-term exam grades, they will have to live with the reality that most of them were acing the course, Lou thought solemnly.

TEN

International balloon champion Doug Wilson was an early riser. After dressing and splashing his face with water, he would leave his motel room and find the closest Starbucks coffee shop. Then, he would return with a copy of USA Today and hot coffee for his morning ritual of reading and enjoying the warm pick-me-up.

On the morning of October 10, a nondescript figure parked in Doug's motel lot, waiting in the car for Doug to keep to his routine. At 6:07 a.m. Doug got in his car and drove off. The silent driver moved his car, backing into an empty slot next to where Doug had been parked. The driver slouched down and waited.

Fifteen minutes later, Doug pulled nose-first into the same spot he had vacated moments before. As soon as he slammed his car door, the driver of the vehicle next to him quickly opened his door, blocking Doug's progress. He struck Doug's left shoulder with a knife; the blade pierced Doug's tee shirt, penetrated soft skin, and pushed into mid-chest, severing the aorta. Doug slumped to the ground, blood and spilled coffee mixing in a sickly brown puddle. Doug Wilson was dead before he knew what hit him. There was little struggle, no shouting or gasping. The knife went in, Doug went down, and in seconds the man was dead.

The murderer quickly took Doug's wallet, got back into his car, and drove away. A few people packing bags into their car trunk nearby didn't notice anything out of the ordinary. The motel clerk did, called 911 and soon thereafter emergency vehicles streamed into the parking lot of the motel.

The media carried out their commitment to get the word to the public. Next morning the following appeared in the Dayton Gazette.

Second Balloon Champion in a Week Murdered

Doug Wilson, a ballooning champion from Chicago, Illinois, was found stabbed to death yesterday morning outside his motel in Dayton, Ohio, where he was preparing for a race. Wilson was known internationally for skillfully guiding his balloon, "Feather," to championships in Europe and the United States. A memorial service is being planned.

Wilson's is the second murder of a champion balloonist within a week. On Saturday, October 2, Janet Reid was killed during an event in Battle Creek. Police have no suspects, but they believe the two murders are related. Members of the ballooning community are in a state of shock to lose two of their biggest crowd-pleasers.

Despite Lou's firm belief that Janet Reid's murder involved Alma College students in some way, a call from Sheriff Pritchard brought a whole new dimension to the case.

"Hi, Lou. I have news about the Reid murder. A major ballooning competitor of Reid's was found dead about an hour ago in Ohio."

"Hmmm, that shifts the energy a bit for me."

"The cause of Doug Wilson's death is plain and simple. He was stabbed to death outside his motel room north of Dayton, Ohio, the site of the next balloon competition."

"Any suspects?"

"None that they know of yet."

"This could be related to Reid's murder, or separate from it," Lou added.

"Yes. Two champion ballooning professionals murdered within days of one another hardly seems like chance."

"True, but Alma students killing both of them also is highly unlikely."

"I agree, but now we have a double murder in the ballooning world."

"Just when I thought Reid's suspect pool was limited to a group of kids, you drop another element into the mix," Lou sighed.

"Sorry Lou, I just thought you ought to know what I know."

Lou called Jack to inform him of the latest development. Nearing the end of his summary, Lou said, "Obviously, whoever murdered Reid had an issue with some part of her life. So, we need to know as much as possible about this woman. Would you take this on, Jack?"

"I told you on the pier at the beginning of your work on the lighthouse murders that I am Sancho. You say 'Jump,' and I'll ask 'How high?' I'll know this Dr. Reid almost better than she knew herself. It may take a little time, but you'll have all you need."

"Thanks, that would be a big help," Lou said. "Perhaps you should contact Dr. Dykstra. He was helpful to me at the funeral, and I'm sure he could get you started. Also, Dean Atkins will cooperate. You'll probably have your own plan, so I'll just leave you to it."

Several hours later, Jack called Lou on his cell. "Want to know what I've learned about Janet Reid, or shall I wait till I have a complete report?"

"Tell me what you know."

"This woman seemed to thrive on controversy. Before Alma, she taught at Lake Superior State University. She was faculty sponsor for the Delta Sigma Rho sorority, which became the target of disciplinary action by the University for serving alcohol on campus and other infractions of Greek policies. Janet Reid informed school officials of the infractions. The sorority sisters saw her as a traitor and made threats against her."

"That was how long ago?" Lou asked.

"In 2005."

"Hmmm, there could be a connection. We'll put that in our back pocket and see how the investigation goes. Why did she leave Lake Superior State for Alma?"

"I don't know that yet."

"Anything else?" Lou asked.

"One item: a professor was denied tenure at Lake Superior State as a result of Reid's poor evaluation of him."

"This woman apparently attracted trouble. What happened to the prof who was denied tenure?"

"I only know he's no longer on staff at Lake Superior State."

"Anything else?"

"One more thing you should know: I must be legit now because I've received my first threat as your assistant."

"How's that, Jack?"

"It was a phone message, a woman's voice, to leave the investigation alone, or I'd regret it."

"Thanks for telling me," Lou said, concerned for his friend. "You want to step aside?"

"No way! Run from a little threat?" You don't, and neither will I."

"Listen, there are a lot of crazy people out there," Lou cautioned. "You can't be too cautious. I don't want any harm coming to you because you teamed with me on an investigation."

"Have you received threats in past investigations?" Jack asked.

"Several times. It goes with the territory."

"Well, then, I can relate to my hero. We go forward."

"Does Elaine know about the threat?" Lou asked.

"No, and she doesn't need to know."

"Okay. Your relationship is what it is," Lou said, not wanting to interfere in how two people communicate. "Thanks. This Lake Superior State angle might break the case."

"I'm back to work, Lou."

"Thanks for the call."

Sheriff Pritchard called Lou to relay a message from Dayton. "Police Chief Bill Upleger thinks, and I agree, that we need to work together on Wilson's murder. The two cases have to be related."

"Very likely. Did you tell him Jack and I were on the case?"

"Yes. He knows how to contact you." Sheriff Pritchard rattled off a Dayton phone number.

"Got it. How was Wilson killed?" Lou asked.

"Stabbed outside his motel room."

"Man, oh, man, those balloonists must be fierce competitors," Lou noted. "The murderer could be someone who always came in third," Lou mused.

"Could be anyone at this point."

"Okay, I'll let Jack know our team has expanded."

"Thanks," Sheriff Pritchard replied. "Stay in touch."

Lou arranged to talk with Bert Dugan, whom he had observed apparently plotting with Sue Starmann before the informal class meeting. Bert was at home in Rockford, Michigan, so they set up a rendezvous at McDonald's, off the Rockford Exit of US-131.

"Thanks for meeting with me," Lou began.

"Sure. I'm curious," Bert replied. "What do you think I can do for you?"

"I have some questions concerning our meeting with your class-mates at Alma," Lou said. "You know, the meeting where Suzanne Starmann confessed to the arson and murder."

"Yeah, that was a real shock! She's the last person I thought would do anything like that."

"You really think she did it?" Lou asked.

"She said she did, so I guess she did," Bert replied. "I really feel sorry for her. Her life is ruined."

"She said she did it for her classmates."

"It was all for nothing, but I suppose we should be grateful."

"Grateful she killed someone?" Lou asked, surprised.

"Well, I didn't mean it that way. I meant grateful that someone would ruin her own life to help the rest of us."

"Did you know she planned to confess at that class meeting?" Lou asked.

"There was a rumor someone might, but I never thought she would do it or that she was guilty."

"Before the meeting, I noticed you talking seriously with her. What was that about?"

"I don't recall. I talked to several people. It was a stressful time."

"Well, you carried on a long conversation with her, and I'm guessing you were trying to talk her out of confessing."

"No, I didn't do that."

"Then what were you talking about?" Lou asked.

After a tell-tale pause, Bert turned away. "I don't think I want to answer that question. I didn't know this was going to be an interrogation. I thought you just wanted to talk about Dr. Reid and Alma College."

"I wouldn't call this an interrogation, Bert. It's no secret that I'm investigating the murder for the Calhoun County sheriff, but I'm only asking questions. I'm a private detective, not an officer of the law."

"You're asking questions about things that are difficult for me to discuss. It almost sounds like I should ask for an attorney."

"That's your right. If you think you need an attorney, and you're not sure what to tell me, you should remain silent." Lou resumed his questioning. "Can I ask about Dr. Reid?"

"I suppose. What do you want to know?"

"I understand she failed most of the students in your chemistry class."

"Yes, that's right."

"Did she return exams with grades on them?"

"Yes, and she told us we all failed. Well, except for Sherry Parker, who got a C-minus."

"Did any of you see an official grade?" Lou asked.

"No. The grades come in the campus mail, probably in the next day or two, but we won't receive grades for chemistry because of the fire."

"You know that for a fact?" Lou asked.

"Well, I assume the fire destroyed all the exams and records in Dr. Reid's office." Bert appeared puzzled.

"Well, no doubt it did, but Dr. Reid had turned in her grades to the Registrar before the fire. They've been recorded."

"Oh, my God!"

"This is news to you?" Lou asked.

"Well, yes. We were under the impression that her records were destroyed."

"Did it occur to you that professors carry important papers in their briefcases or keep them in home offices? Quite frankly, to think burning an office would destroy all important papers is naïve."

Bert sat staring at the table, shaking his head.

"Did your class plot to torch your professor's office, Bert?" Lou asked outright.

"No, we didn't."

"Are you willing to take a polygraph test if the authorities ask for one?"

"I think I want to talk to a lawyer first. But no, we did not plot to burn her office. Suzanne confessed to it. If she did it, she acted alone."

"Bert, I'm confident that Suzanne did not set fire to Dr. Reid's office."

"I don't know if she did it!" Bert said. "The class did not plot to do it, and that's true!"

Lou resumed calmly. "Let me level with you, Bert. When I saw you talking with Suzanne before the class meeting, the word 'strategy' came to mind. I believed the two of you were discussing a plan. When she confessed, I immediately thought you were in on it, recalling your serious talk with her."

"We were not talking about a confession."

"Okay. Bert, is Suzanne Starmann a member of your chemistry class?"

"Yes. I suppose…"

"Then why isn't she listed as a student on the official enrollment record?" Lou asked.

"She's auditing the class. She's not taking it for credit."

"So, she's not getting a grade, right?"

"Right."

"Then why would she care what grade she received, and why should she torch an office and kill a professor? The class won't impact her overall grade point average, nor will it jeopardize her getting into graduate school."

"I guess she's a martyr. If she did it, she did it for us."

"Did what exactly?" Lou asked.

"Set fire to Dr. Reid's office."

"Did she kill the professor?"

"She maintains she did, so I guess she did."

"Thanks for talking with me, Bert," Lou said, reaching out to shake Bert's hand. "If you have anything else to tell me, please call."

"I will."

ELEVEN

The three-member chase crew for Janet Reid met for dinner at the Oasis Bar on 28th Street in S.E. Grand Rapids. Linda Ross, Barry Sims, and Pat True sat in the bar waiting for a table. They wasted no time getting to what was on their minds.

"Well, Linda, I see you killed Doug," Pat offered.

"I didn't kill him!" Linda responded sharply.

"Oh, come on, don't give me that! You said you were going to do it."

"Stab a big guy like that? No way! He could snap me like a wooden match."

"Well, sometimes prayers are answered," Pat replied. "I'm really thankful, Linda, very thankful!"

"So, maybe you hired a hit man?" Barry asked.

"I didn't kill Doug!" Linda paused for breath. "I finally came to my senses. I thought Janet would want me to avenge her murder, but later I realized it was stupid of me to throw away my life when Janet can't appreciate my actions."

"Who killed Wilson then?" Barry asked.

"I haven't a clue," Linda replied, disgusted.

Jack called Lou. "Hi! I've got more on Janet Reid."

"She was hiding under the Witness Protection Program?" Lou replied scarcastically.

"No," said Jack with a chuckle.

"A CIA spy?" Lou asked.

"Nope, but she was the debate coach at Alma."

"Of course," Lou replied. "How much conflict can there be on a debate team?"

"Plenty. Debate coaches in the conference had little respect for her. They think she was cheating."

"What? How do you cheat on a debate team?" Lou asked.

"You asked me to find out about the woman," Jack replied, a bit upset that Lou was not taking his research seriously. "I can't figure all the ins and outs of her personality, likes and dislikes."

"I was merely asking a rhetorical question. I didn't expect you to answer it. We'll add this to her profile, but I doubt coaching debate figures into her murder."

"You never know when a bit of information can turn a case around," Jack said.

"You are right, Jack, you never know," Lou replied. "I was on the Alma College debate team back in 1960 — or maybe it was '61. We had some intense rivalries within the state, and also against West Point and Notre Dame."

"Well, there's a coincidence," Jack replied. "I was on the debate team at Aquinas."

"No way!"

"I sure was," Jack replied. "I had my card box of quotes and statistics. My partner saved us time after time."

"You weren't so fast in thinking of responses to the opponent's comments?" Lou asked with a smile.

"Not really. My partner would slip me a quote or two when it was my turn to rebut, and I would then wax eloquent for the allowed time. Most of the time the judges were impressed with my presentation, but the cards my partner slipped me were really the deciding factor." Jack appeared rueful.

"My partner, Gary Miller, was the intellectual who played a similar role on our team," Lou admitted. "I was a good speaker, but he was the brains of the duo."

"That makes us a couple of losers, Lou."

"That's one way to look at it, but I'd rather view us as analytical types," Lou countered. "We may not have been fast, but we could see the big picture. In a debate, your opponent is alive, and in our work, the opponent, in a sense, is dead, or playing hard-to-get. In solving murders, we may have trouble fitting together the obvious clues, but in the long run, we figure it out."

"Sort of gives us an advantage, if you ask me," Jack said with a smile

"Well, let's just say that we haven't lost a match yet."

Lou contacted John Ickes, the director of the Battle Creek Air Balloon Festival.

"Mr. Ickes, this is Lou Searing. I'm assisting Sheriff Pritchard in looking into the murder of Janet Reid."

"Yes, I know of you by reputation. I'm relieved you and Mr. Kelly are working on this terrible crime."

"I don't mean to sound boastful, but Jack and I will figure it out eventually. I called to see if you have any information that will help us. You may have already answering these questions for Detective Jaggers, and if so, just tell me."

"I haven't talked to anyone from the sheriff's office yet. I'll help if I can."

"Thanks. To begin with, is there a record of everyone who came to the balloon festival?"

"No. We record ticket sales, but we have no way of knowing people by name."

"Okay, then let me ask…"

"Wait a minute," John interrupted. "I should explain. If someone buys a ticket on the Internet, then, yes, we know who purchased the ticket. But someone buying tickets at the gate, or at one of our cooperating businesses — no, we wouldn't know who came to the show."

"Was any security video taken before or during the show, like at the gate, or around the area where the balloons were preparing for ascent?"

"No, we don't have any security cameras. The balloonmeister and my staff only allow pilots and their crews into the lift-area, and they, as well as the media reps, have badges which are checked by our security staff. People who come to the festival are not screened, nor is any video taken. In retrospect, it would have been a good idea, but a murder connected with our festival was the last thing we considered."

"I understand," Lou said. "Do you know of any violence in the context of ballooning events around the country?"

"No. We're a pretty safe venue. Our people simply love to fly balloons, and they enjoy the fellowship at this type of festival.

Actually, the pilots and crews seem to become one big family. But they do compete, so I imagine with that comes pride, jealousy, and greed. But I know of no history of violence in ballooning."

"I see. Do you know if Janet Reid had any enemies?"

"No. I don't know any of the balloonists well. I had heard of Janet, and of Doug Wilson, because we invited them to our festival. It was a plus for us to have international champions here. Janet won some events at the Albuquerque festival, and Doug has won some prestigious international events. People who know of their reputations would come just to see them, get autographs, and so forth."

"I presume you know that Doug Wilson was murdered while in Dayton at that festival."

"Yes, so sad. Those two, Janet and Doug, were our big draws."

"That covers it for me for today. Thank you, Mr. Ickes," said Lou.

"I'm sorry, Mr. Searing. I don't think I've been of any help to you."

"Sometimes, lack of information has some significance. My partner and I simply put what we learn together and hope a pattern appears."

"Oh, wait a minute!" John said. "I just thought of something. A documentary company sought permission to do a film about ballooning in general, and our festival in particular. A couple of camera crews took clips of various aspects of the festival and the ballooning events. They might have caught something that helps."

"Excellent. What's the company name?" Lou asked.

"Let me check their letterhead from when they asked to film our events."

A few seconds later John came back on the line. "The company is Festivals of America, president is Wendy Coulter." He read off a Cleveland phone number.

"Thanks much, Mr. Ickes. I'll call Miss Coulter and see if she can help. If you learn anything else that might help, please let me know."

"Sure. Once you solve it, I'll take you and your partner for a ride. Have you ever been up in a balloon before?"

"No, but thanks a lot. We'll take you up on your offer, pun intended."

Lou called Jack. "I talked with the festival director. His reward for our solving Reid's murder will be a balloon ride. You game?"

"Sure. Sounds like fun."

"I also learned something helpful. I'd like you to go to Cleveland for some sleuthing. Can you get away for a couple of days?"

"Whatever you need, Lou. Cleveland… hmmm. Maybe next time you could send me to Hawaii, or Bermuda?"

"What do you have against Cleveland, Jack?"

"Nothing. Rock and Roll Hall of Fame and a new ball park — if I have some spare time, I'm going to visit those for sure. But why am I going there?"

"A video company filmed the Battle Creek Festival for a documentary. Once I contact them, I'd like you to review their film from Battle Creek to check for suspicious activity. It might be wise to take along photos of the Alma students, especially Suzanne Starmann."

"Do you want this done as soon as yesterday?" Jack asked.

"If possible." Lou said with a smile, "Can you go tomorrow?"

"Yes. Unless Elaine has plans, I'm free."

"Let me know if there is a conflict. I'll call you back as soon as I get permission for you to review the film. I'll either call or leave a message on your cell."

"Thanks, Lou. I don't doubt that I'll see the murderer at some point in the film."

Chief Upleger called Lou from Dayton. "There've been some interesting developments in the murder of Doug Wilson. Are you making any progress?"

"Nothing is popping out on the Reid murder," Lou replied. "I'm glad you're having some luck. What have you found?"

"We have the car that we think was involved. There are blood drops matching Wilson's blood type and several clear fingerprints. We also found flyers for the Dayton festival and a typewritten, probably computer-generated, note that Wilson would be staying at the Comfort Inn."

"Who owns the car?"

"Jim White, a member of Wilson's chase team."

"Really?"

"Our first suspects were his chase team. We looked into each person's background, including car registration and past involvement with the law. White's car was at the Dayton festival. We got a search warrant and found the blood, fingerprints, and papers."

"But you've no direct evidence that he killed Wilson, do you?"

"No, but we picked him up on suspicion of murder."

"He denies involvement, I presume?" Lou asked.

"Absolutely. Has no idea how blood got in his car. He has an alibi for when Wilson was killed, and it seems to be sticking."

"Any evidence the car was at the scene of the murder? A witness, or security video?"

"Not yet. As I said, we think the car was used. But who was in it, and was it stolen and returned? Lots of questions, Lou."

"Going to do polygraph on this White?"

"I doubt it — not right away. He's retained a good lawyer. We'll keep digging into his background for a motive for his wanting Wilson dead."

Over the phone, Jack presented Lou with a theory. "I think we need to expand our suspect pool beyond Alma College students and the ballooning community."

"Who do you have in mind, Jack?"

"Parents."

"Go on."

"Alma students are extensions of their parents. The students' aspirations, successes, and failures are the parents' as well. If a student had a motive for revenge, the parents might have felt a stronger urge."

"I see your point," Lou replied. "In that sense, a parent may have a greater motive to see that Reid's grades didn't reach the Registrar."

"I agree. They wouldn't want to see their kid's future messed up because of a low grade or the questions that might arise in the minds of the people reviewing grad-school applications. With so many undergrads applying with straight A's, one bad grade could tip the scale in the direction of another applicant."

"Right. Whether a kid gets into medical school could hinge on that grade, for instance."

"Or, maybe not just acceptance, but Harvard Law School versus Michigan State University."

"So, I suppose we should look at the parents and check their alibis."

"Right. It's a lot of work, but it has to be done."

Dean Atkins provided home addresses for the eleven students in Chemistry 231. Because of the crisis on campus, the dean had come in contact with most of the parents of students in the class. In addition, the Dean gave Lou and Jack his initial impressions of the parents. He was confident that only two of them could be involved: Becky Mulligan's father and Patty McIntyre's mother. Both had verbally threatened Dr. Reid's life after their daughters told them of the failing grades.

During irate telephone calls to Dean Atkins, Mr. Mulligan had said something to the effect of, "If my daughter fails the class, that prof will be pushing up daisies!" Mrs. McIntyre offered a similar threat: "Failing my daughter will have chilling consequences for the instructor!!" The dean was certain the comments had been made in extreme anger, but all threats needed to be taken seriously.

Lou called on Harold and Cynthia McIntyre in Allegan the evening of October 7. He arrived unannounced because he wanted to note their responses and behaviors after his introduction. When Harold McIntyre answered his knock, Lou began, "Mr. McIntyre? I'm Lou Searing. I'm helping the Calhoun County Sheriff, Michael Pritchard, solve the murder of Dr. Reid. May I have a word with you?"

"We have a church meeting, but we have a few minutes. Come in." If Lou had expected surprise or shock, it wasn't evident.

"Thank you."

Lou was shown into the living room. As he sat down, a calico cat rubbed against his ankle, reminding him of Millie's solicitous foot-rubs at home.

"How can we help you?" Cynthia McIntyre asked, entering the living room. She moved with the aid of a walker and sat down in a straight-backed chair.

"We're talking with anyone who might have information about this crime. Naturally, the parents of the students taking chemistry from Dr. Reid have a lot at stake with their children's grades."

"Where are you going with this, Mr. Searing?" Harold asked. "Are you insinuating that we killed Dr. Reid?"

"We have no definite suspects, but we're gathering information. Your daughter Patty is in the class, so you might help us understand Dr. Reid or the circumstances surrounding her death."

"From what we gather from Patty, this professor was an evil person. I'm shocked that someone with her cruel personality was hired to teach at a school as prestigious as Alma," Cynthia said forcefully.

"I agree," Harold added. "She appeared to have no understanding of psychology. No reporting to the dean that students were failing, no indication to the students, no indication to parents. Out of the blue, the kids get frightening news of impending failure. That's no way to teach a class, interact with young people, or represent an employer."

"As a former educator, I agree," Lou replied. "What did you do when you heard this news?"

"I called the dean," Cynthia said, "within five minutes of Patty's report, I think. I was quite emotional, said some things I regret. But my point was that I was angry and felt I had a right to be. We pay tuition for Patty to gain a quality education, not to be treated like a silly coed."

"Did the parents band together?" Lou asked.

"No," Harold replied. "There were a few calls between families, but there was no meeting or collective discussion."

"I see."

"I believe you think we were more involved, Mr. Searing," Harold said suspiciously. "Why else would you make the effort to drive here instead of calling us on the phone? If you suspect us, tell us, so we can defend ourselves."

"I understand your thinking," Lou replied. "But murder requires thorough investigation. I talked with Dean Atkins about parent reactions to Dr. Reid's classroom announcement to the students. He was confident that no parent was involved in the murder, but he shared all threatening statements he heard. You, Mrs. McIntyre, purportedly made a threatening statement, so I had an obligation to make sure that you were not involved in Dr. Reid's murder."

"I was not!" Cynthia replied vehemently. "I'm certain that if you give me a specific time-frame, I could provide a reasonable alibi. My word may not be sufficient, but I did not kill the woman. Yes, I made a threatening statement to Dean Atkins. I was angry, but I did not commit murder, nor could I ever do such a thing."

Before Lou had started his car, Harold McIntyre was on the phone to Mike Mulligan.

"Has Lou Searing talked to you? He's a private detective working on the Reid murder."

"Haven't heard from him. Who's he working for?" Mike asked.

"Doesn't matter. He's good, and he may want to talk to you. He knew Cynthia threatened Reid when she talked to Dean Atkins. So did you, so I imagine he'll be knocking on your door soon."

"What should I tell him?" Mike asked.

"Whatever you want. Just don't give him anything that would lead him to look deeper, at least not in terms of our involvement."

"Will he want to know where I was at certain times?" Mike asked.

"Probably. That's what Cynthia has to give him."

"So, now what do I do?"

"Figure something out — in a hurry!"

Michael Mulligan, the second parent to be interviewed, was single and living in North Muskegon. Lou called first, because he needed some assurance that his suspect would be available. They agreed on a time at Mr. B's Pancake House, and as was Lou's habit, he was early for the meeting.

Lou chose a table near the window so he could watch Mr. Mulligan arrive. Often, Lou could glean much from body-position, facial expression, and demeanor before or during a meeting.

A few minutes early, a car pulled into a parking space across the street, and a middle-aged man got out and stood by the vehicle. He lit a cigarette and began to pace back and forth, as if nervously anticipating a confrontation. Then the man abruptly dropped the

cigarette on the ground, stomped on it with his right foot, and pro-
ceeded to cross the street. He entered the restaurant, apparently
looking for someone matching Lou's description. He spotted Lou by
the window and approached.

"Mr. Searing?"

"Yes. Mr. Mulligan?"

"I'm a little early. Hope you don't mind."

"That's fine. The sooner we begin, the sooner we finish," Lou
said, trying to put Mr. Mulligan at ease.

"Good. Listen, I'm really nervous about this. I have nothing to be
nervous about, but for some reason I'm a basket case."

"You're worried about being interviewed by a detective?" Lou
asked. Mr. Mulligan nodded.

"Well, you needn't be. Please sit down. Think of me simply as
a former Alma student who is helping out in the investigation of
Dr. Reid's murder. I'm not the police, the FBI, or the CIA. I'm just a
friend of the college who wants to help during this upsetting time."

"Intellectually, I know that," Mike said, as he sat down across the
table from Lou. "But I've seen too many television shows where they
get people to say things they shouldn't say, or that maybe aren't even
true. I'm afraid that might happen to me."

"All I'm looking for is the truth, which shouldn't be threatening,
unless you're involved in the fire or the murder."

"No, I'm not!"

"Well, then you have nothing to fear. I don't I think you committed a crime, but you threatened Dr. Reid, and that's cause for me to
seek you out."

"I know, I lost my temper. My daughter Becky was very upset
with this professor, and after her mother and I divorced I promised
her that I would protect her and try to be a good father. So, upsetting

Becky is like upsetting me. You simply don't treat my daughter this way and not face consequences."

"By consequences you mean…"

"Meaning firing, or a reprimand from the president. At least offering a second examination over material in the syllabus or in lectures."

"How about murder?"

"Mr. Searing, murder is a mortal sin. Believe me, venial sins are my specialty, but mortal sins are missing from my repertoire of ways to distance myself from God and the Holy Spirit."

"So, I take it you were not involved with either the fire or the murder?" Lou asked.

"Not the murder. But, I was an accessory to the fire."

"Accessory?" Lou said, surprised at the confession.

"I supplied advice."

"To whom?" Lou asked.

"I will not say," Mike said. "Not without an attorney. At this point, I will only admit to being involved in the fire, and my involvement was only in giving advice. But apparently it was followed, given that a fire burned Dr. Reid's office and lab."

"Did you talk with anyone before offering this advice?" Lou asked. "I mean, did a group of parents plot this?"

"I will not answer that."

"Which means you did?"

"No, which means I will not answer your question."

Lou took a deep breath. "The person you offered the advice to — was he or she a student? A parent?"

Mr. Mulligan shook his head. "Look, I told you I was involved, and I'm prepared to accept responsibility as accessory to the crime of arson. But I will not tell you whom I advised nor the nature of my advice. I am probably stupid to admit my involvement, but I was raised to be honest. So I told you."

"I appreciate your honesty, and I respect your not wanting to give me any further information. Let me ask this: do you know who set fire to the office?"

"I know to whom I gave advice, but I don't know if he carried it out."

"Do you know who killed Dr. Reid?" Lou asked.

"No, I don't. I was led to believe that torching the woman's office would destroy the grading sheet and probably scare her into being fair with the kids. The fire was meant to wake up the administration to the fact that they had a major problem with a faculty member. I tell you, I did not participate, know of, or even hear talk of any violence toward the woman. Torching her office, yes; murder, no."

"Thank you, Mr. Mulligan. Here is my card, in case you want to tell me more." Lou walked away, confused. He had taken the fire marshal's report as gospel, but now he had reason to doubt that. Perhaps the fire was not an accident after all.

Mike was angry with himself for admitting complicity in torching Dr. Reid's office. He realized that any attorney worth his salt would certainly have advised against doing so. And he knew that, once he called his attorney, he would be reprimanded, and deservedly so.

Lou now had an Alma connection to the fire, if not to the murder. He called Jack.

"Mr. Mulligan admits he was involved with the fire in Reid's office, but not with the murder. He sounded convincing, and I believe him. He may know who killed Reid, but I'm pretty sure he wasn't involved in the murder."

"Hmmm, interesting."

"He said he advised someone regarding the arson, but he wouldn't tell me who."

"Was his attorney around?" Jack asked.

"No."

"Ouch!"

"Ouch what?" Lou asked.

"Ouch, as in the attorney will do everything and anything to have anything Mr. Mulligan told you thrown out."

"I'm not an officer of the law, and I wasn't talking with him in any official capacity," Lou said.

"True, but the judge may not buy that."

"I imagine you're right. Well, that's for the prosecutor to deal with. All I know is that man's admission helps in our investigation. I happen to believe him; to me either the fire was the act of Alma students, or of Alma parents, or those responsible for the fire are connected to Alma in some way."

"Good, Lou! That means we have Suzanne, a student, admitting to setting fire to the office of the professor, and Mr. Mulligan, a parent, but not her parent, admitting to being an accessory to the arson."

"Correct, and I'm fairly certain that Suzanne is not the arsonist nor the murderer. Back to work, Jack! I just wanted to keep you informed."

"Thanks. Now, can I tell you what I've learned?"

"Go ahead."

"I'm in Cleveland, you'll recall."

"Oh, yes, reviewing the film of the Battle Creek Ballooning Festival."

"Yes. People here have been very cooperative."

"That's good to hear. What have you found?" Lou asked.

"You won't like it, but here goes. The only thing I can see in the video is Reid's balloon, uninflated, lying on its side. In the distance is a person who appears to be rising after being inside or very near the wicker basket, which is also on its side."

"Great. Who is it?"

"I haven't a clue. You can't see the face, and it's only visible for a few seconds."

"Is this person a man or a woman?"

"I'm not sure."

"Could you see enough for any identification — hair color, hair length, height of the person, age? Anything?"

"You can judge for yourself when you see it. If I had to guess, I'd say it is an older man, but he doesn't move suspiciously. You just see the person rise, as if in some pain, back to the camera, and calmly walk away."

"Can you see Suzanne Starmann anywhere near Reid before lift-off or during the unfolding, while the balloon is being inflated?"

"No. Reid can be seen from a distance talking to some people, but none of them appear to be Suzanne."

"Well, good. That helps," Lou said.

"That helps?" Jack asked, confused. "I didn't find anything that helps."

"Seeing nothing is sometimes seeing a lot. Your observation supports my contention that Suzanne is lying. The video indicates that a male may have interfered with the propane tank. Be sure to get a copy of that portion of the video. I think the prosecutor will be very happy with it, and perhaps your findings will tip the scale in convicting the murderer."

"If you say so. I'm heading home in a few hours. You can reach me on the cell of course, but I should be home around eleven or so."

"Safe journey, Jack, and thanks a lot!"

TWELVE

Lou called Dayton Police Chief Bill Upleger daily to check on the Wilson investigation. Most days there was nothing to report but today was different.

"Thanks for calling, Lou. We've been talking with several people about Wilson's background," Chief Upleger said. "No surprises with this guy — wore his life on his sleeve. There doesn't seem to be anyone in his life with reason to kill him."

"Anybody worth his salt has at least one person who has an issue with him," Lou responded, chuckling.

"Precisely; that's why I have something for you."

"Are you are about to pull a skeleton from the closet?" Lou asked.

"I suppose you could say that. During our third interview with Wilson's wife, we learned that he deeply mistrusted Jim White, a member of his chase crew."

"What was the source of the mistrust? Jealousy?"

"Well, his fear bordered on paranoia. I'm no doctor, but apparently Wilson considered Jim White a real threat. Wilson had a problem with his balloon a year ago, and he believed White was responsible for the miscue. Had Wilson not uncovered the error, he could easily have been killed."

"That would do it."

"White was adamant he had nothing to do with the error. The two had a knock-down, drag-out fight over it, but eventually the other crew members helped them get back on speaking terms."

"Why didn't Wilson just tell him to take a walk?" Lou asked.

"They had been lifelong friends, and Mrs. Wilson says that her husband was once treated for paranoia. She convinced him that White wasn't the threat Doug perceived him to be."

"So, now we truly have White as a suspect in Wilson's murder, and you've got blood in his car and other incriminating evidence."

"Yes, but White has an alibi. I think someone who wanted Wilson dead knew of the confrontation between the two men and used the fight to throw suspicion on Jim."

"Possible, I guess. Who might this someone be?" Lou asked.

"A member of Janet Reid's chase crew. Doug and Janet were strong competitors, and every race was contentious. In one way it was immature, but in another way, any competition brought out a strong will to win, to defeat the enemy, so to speak."

"Balloon events?" Lou replied, a bit astounded.

"Competition is competition, Lou. It could happen over playing marbles, I suppose."

"So, you're saying a member of the Reid support crew, believing that Wilson killed Reid, killed Wilson in revenge, and in doing so, set up this Jim White guy."

"Stranger things have happened."

"Are you planning to pursue this?" Lou asked.

"We'll look into it, yes."

"Please keep me posted."

Jack followed up on the lead regarding Dr. Reid's history at Lake Superior State University. He visited with the housemother of the Delta Sigma Rho sorority, Mrs. Cece Brigham, in the common room of the sorority house.

"Thank you for meeting with me, Mrs. Brigham."

"I'm happy to talk with you, Mr. Kelly. I knew Janet Reid would meet her fate sooner or later," Cece began with fiery emotion. "I could smell trouble from the moment I met her!"

"Why do you say that, Mrs. Brigham?"

"The older I get, the more I learn to trust my instincts. At 83, I've had a lot of experience dealing with people of all ages. After a while, you get so that when you smell a rat, you know it's a rat. And, with this woman, I smelled a rat."

"I respect your intuition, but why did you smell trouble?" Jack asked.

"She was full of herself. She had just gotten her Ph.D, and she hadn't a humble bone in her body. You see, some intellectuals, when they get these degrees, recognize that all they did was go to school for three more years. If they are honest, they admit they know even less than when they started the program. Others seem to think God has just given them membership in Heaven. They insist on being called 'Doctor.' They have to be admired, not just respected, and have a holier-than-thou attitude. That was Janet Reid when I met her. She probably always wanted to be a medical doctor, but she couldn't get into medical school. She pursued a Ph.D. so she could be called 'Doctor Reid' for the rest of her life."

"I see. And this contributed to her troubles here at Lake Superior State?" Jack asked.

"Certainly. As you know, she reported this sorority to the administration for a drinking violation and several other minor infractions."

"Isn't that what she should do?" Jack asked.

"Mr. Kelly, I don't condone underage drinking, and I believe in following university and Greek rules and guidelines. But you don't just walk into the administration building making wild claims, getting people in trouble. You try to work things out at the level of the problem. You see, that was the trouble with her. She didn't have the students' best interests at heart. She didn't think before she acted."

"It sounds like you were letting your sorority get away with illegal behavior."

"That is not true! The Dean of Women will tell you that I had given her a full report. The dean trusted me to do what I could to turn things around in the sorority. We were putting together a plan to take care of the problem. But, no, Janet Reid went first to the campus newspaper and that's the worst thing you can do! Then she still didn't go through channels. She went straight to the President of the Board of Regents — didn't even talk to the dean, who could have told her it was being handled."

"I see what you mean."

"Thank you. Then you have the unintended consequences of the behavior."

"Like what?" Jack asked.

"Like youngsters having their college careers tarnished. Reports went into student files, reports which will harm students' chances when they try to get into graduate schools or find a job. The aftermath of her inappropriate actions was terrifying."

"Were any threats made against her life?" Jack asked.

"Is she still teaching here?" Cece said with a smile on her face.

"No."

"Well, there. Need I say more?"

"I guess not. Could someone in Delta Sigma Rho have killed Dr. Reid?" Jack asked, getting right to the point.

"Sure. Some girls will never forgive her."

"Really?"

"Really, and I don't blame them. I've tried to help them get past this, but the woman brought it on herself, Mr. Kelly. She really did."

Jack paused, and then spoke carefully. "Let me try to understand, not to misquote you. You think someone from this sorority could possibly have killed Dr. Reid?"

"I have no evidence, only my intuition. I simply say, Janet Reid wreaked havoc in this sorority, and it's possible that someone — or more than one — might have wanted her dead."

"I understand. Thank you."

Things had quieted on the Alma College campus. Word was that Suzanne had admitted to setting the fire and killing Dr. Reid, and as far as most people were concerned, it was wrapped up. But, they were wrong. Lou and Jack, among others, were confident that Suzanne was simply exhibiting her Obsessive Compulsive Disorder, and now a sorority in Michigan's Upper Peninsula might be involved in the case. In addition, a parent not connected to Sue had admitted to being an accessory to the fire. So, the calm was only a brief respite after the flurry of activity following the campus fire and the murder.

The Registrar had sent out the grades and, as Chemistry 231 students opened the letter and grade reports from the Registrar,

most found an A for Dr. Reid's class. The only exception was Don
Collins: Dr. Reid had given him a D.

The ten who received A's presumed that the college had mandated
the grades as recompense for what the students had been through in
the last week. But, slowly word spread that the high grades had been
assigned by Dr. Reid and were her actual evaluations of the students'
work in her class.

THIRTEEN

At home in Grand Haven, Lou's phone rang. "Lou Searing."

"Lou, this is Maggie McMillan."

"Oh my goodness, it's wonderful to hear from you!!"

"Thank you. Happy Birthday, Lou."

"Thank you for remembering. Yes, I'm 67 today."

"Just a youngster."

"Compared to Methuselah, I am, but by any other yardstick, I'm getting up there, Maggie."

Maggie, a wheel-chair user, had helped Lou solve a number of murders over the last ten years. She stopped working with Lou when she and her dentist husband Tom adopted a baby from Korea. Maggie wisely concluded that putting herself in harm's way was not the best behavior for a mother now responsible for raising an infant daughter.

"First of all, I'm doing fine. My daughter, LuLing, is sitting up, talking — well, okay, babbling — but she's simply delightful."

"You like being a mother, I gather."

"Love it, Lou. LuLing brings us so much joy."

"That's wonderful. Your being a chair-user isn't a problem?"

"Not yet. The house is barrier-free as you know, and I have most things at a low level — crib, changing table, and so on."

"Marvelous."

"Lou, I called because I want to become involved again. Raising a daughter is great, but I long for the mental stimulation of helping you solve a challenging case."

"Have you heard that Jack Kelly has joined me?"

"I read about him in The Lighthouse Murders. I didn't know if he was a real person or simply a character from the deepest part of your imagination."

"No, he's a real person, and a real character as well."

"If you two interact as well in real life as you do in the book, you're lucky to have each other."

"Yes, it's working out quite well, but that doesn't mean you can't join us. In fact several readers have asked, 'Where's Maggie?'"

"But, maybe three's a crowd."

"Not when it comes to solving a complicated murder, and the current case is complicated."

"You're so kind. I can't be an on-the-scene person, but if you two could use some other help, I'd love to do research, or think, or plot and plan, if you two would have me."

"I'll talk to Jack, but I can't imagine he'd mind."

"Thanks, Lou. I really do miss you and Carol, Millie and Samm, and getting my nose into fact-finding."

"We miss you too, Maggie. You'll hear from me."

Once Jack heard about Suzanne's diagnosis of OCD, he said to Lou, "I think we need to learn more about this mental health disorder."

"I agree. Do you want to look into it?" Lou asked.

"I suppose I could, if you'll direct me where to start."

"Just a minute! I got a call from Maggie. She'd like to help us by working in the background."

"That's great!" Jack replied.

"I think I'll ask her to become our mental health consultant."

"Ours?" Jack said with a chuckle.

"Granted, we could use it, but I was referring to…"

"I know. I'm just trying to add a little humor here."

Lou dialed Maggie's number. When she answered, he began, "We've got some work for you to do."

"I'm ready. What do you need?"

"We have a suspect, a coed who has admitted to torching a chemistry prof's office and then murdering her. However, I talked with a psychiatrist who is treating her. She gave him her permission to explain that he's certain she's suffering from OCD and didn't commit either crime. Quite frankly, I believe him. That being said, Jack and I still need to understand OCD."

"That's something I can research."

"Great. Jack or I could go to the Internet and supposedly become experts in a matter of minutes. But I need someone who can access all the resources, then relay the details to me at my level, in language I can understand."

"Being a dentist, Tom has a lot of medical friends. Maybe I can sit down with a psychiatrist and learn about this from a specialist."

"Whatever you can do, Maggie. I need to understand and you can help by teaching me."

"I'm going to work. Thanks, Lou."

Maggie immediately called Heather Moore, a sixteen-year-old junior at Battle Creek Central High School. Heather was doing well in school, but like Maggie, Heather was a chair-user. She was having difficulty being a pretty teenager and adjusting to life using a wheel-chair. The school counselor had encouraged Heather and Maggie to become acquainted so that Heather could have an adult model for adjusting to a disability.

In return, providing occasional child care for LuLing, Maggie often took Heather to the movies or shopping. But this would be a great opportunity to involve Heather, Maggie thought. She called.

"Heather, I just heard from Mr. Searing. He wants me — and that means us — to help him solve an arson and murder case at Alma College."

"I'm thinking of applying to Alma!" Heather exclaimed.

"Alma is a great school. And, you have the grades to be accepted there."

"Anyway, you were saying we have work to do?" Heather asked.

"Yes, we are to find out all we can about Obsessive Compulsive Disorder."

"I've never even heard of it."

"It means believing something exists or is happening when it isn't real."

"I thought that was an illusion," Heather asked.

"I think an illusion, in the normal sense, is seeing something that isn't there. You know, like a mirage. You think you see water up ahead on a hot road, but it disappears when you get close. That's an illusion. I think OCD, the mental health term, means you not only believe you are seeing something, or that something exists, but you act as if what you see or think really does exist."

"I guess so. Why couldn't Mr. Searing give us something fun?"

Maggie chuckled. "Have you heard the phrase, 'She's compulsive about washing her hands?'"

"Yes."

"Well, that means that someone over-reacts to a situation or believes she is giving way too much attention to something."

"You mean, you think you are in the Garden of Eden when you are really in a patch of weeds," Heather said, with a chuckle.

"I guess so, but you live your life as if you really are in the Garden of Eden."

"I guess I get it, but how does this relate to a fire and murder?" Heather asked.

"A student at Alma says she burned a professor's office and then murdered her, and she's trying to convince others, including the police, that she did. But perhaps she has OCD…"

"Meaning she didn't do it, but she's convinced she did do it, and is living as if she did," Heather replied.

"BINGO! You've got it."

"So, what does Mr. Searing need?" Heather asked.

"We need to learn as much as we can about OCD so we can help him understand how it might relate to the crime."

"Ok, but next time, could we maybe ride along when the criminal is being chased and arrested?" Heather asked hesitantly.

"Well, Heather, I don't want to disappoint you, but being a detective is doing a lot of things that aren't really fun. It's hard work.

Mr. Searing says it's like putting a puzzle together without a picture to work from."

"But when you helped him solve murders, you were where the action was, right?"

"Yes, I was, but action doesn't always translate into fun. Believe me, getting shot isn't fun."

"Is that what caused you to be a chair-user?"

"No, but it could have." Maggie cleared her throat. "Okay, now how do we proceed?" Maggie asked the rhetorical question.

"Go to the Internet?" Heather replied.

"Sure. But, I think we also need to take a psychiatrist to lunch to see if he or she can talk at our level."

"Why take the doctor to lunch?" Heather asked.

"Or breakfast. Lou always says, when one needs information, one should take a knowledgeable person to lunch and ask questions. Everyone likes a free meal and to share what they know."

"That sounds like fun. I'll order a hamburger and pretend I'm eating a salad. We'll see what the doctor has to say about that!" Heather and Maggie shared a good laugh.

On Monday morning, October 11, ten of the eleven Chemistry 231 students gathered in the student union. They had initially planned to meet privately, but that might arouse suspicion, so they chose to meet in the Stewart room in the Student Center. Bert Dugan also had asked Dean Atkins to attend the first part of the meeting and report what progress had been made in solving the murder.

The dean's presentation was short. "I have nothing to report. I will say, however, that the grades you received for your half-semester of chemistry were issued by Professor Reid and were not sympathy grades, as a couple of you have suggested. The grading sheet was not destroyed in the fire. The grades were submitted to the Registrar after the mid-term exams were graded. So, you must have impressed the late professor with your mastery of the subject matter in her class. Are there any questions?"

"Can you tell us if we are still suspects?" Fran Henne asked.

"I can't speak to that. Mr. Searing and Mr. Kelly continue to interview people, and, I haven't heard of any developments beyond Suzanne's admission of guilt."

"Thank you for coming to speak with us, Dean Atkins," Bert Dugan said.

"You're quite welcome." With that, Dean Atkins left the group.

"I've been interviewed by Mr. Searing," Bert stated. "But I don't think I'm a suspect. Has he talked to anyone else?"

"I know he talked to my parents," Patty McIntyre offered.

"I wonder why?" Bert asked.

"Because, after I told them what happened, my mother called Dean Atkins and threatened Dr. Reid. She was pretty upset."

"Mr. Searing has also spoken to my Dad," Becky Mulligan said.

"And why was that?" Bert again asked.

"He also made a threatening comment."

"And I assume both of your parents have been cleared?"

"As far as I know, my parents are no longer suspect," Patty replied.

Becky spoke hesitantly. "I probably shouldn't tell you this, but my father told Mr. Searing he was involved in the arson."

"Was he?" Bert said, while all the students looked in Becky's direction.

"Yes. I don't know all the details. He has a lawyer, and he hasn't told me any more than that."

"This is bad," Bert said. "We agreed to come up with logical explanations of our whereabouts, but we didn't think they'd bring our parents into this. This is not good." The others nodded in agreement.

"Why would he tell Mr. Searing he was in on the arson?" Bert asked. "That makes no sense!"

"I think Mr. Mulligan is a good man," Patty said. "Maybe he's guilt-ridden over what he did, so that he wants to come clean."

"Is that your thinking, Becky?" Bert asked.

"My father's actions are not like him at all. I think he was so upset at what was happening to me that he just lost it for a while. When he had time to think, he probably felt terrible about it and wants to right a wrong, I guess."

"Sherry, has Mr. Searing talked with your parents?"

"No. And I ask them every day, so they would tell me if he had."

"Thank goodness," Bert replied.

The students discussed the amazing turnaround of grades. While they were thankful for justice on the grading, they were still upset with the continued suspicion.

Don Collins had left the Alma College campus following the student meeting to craft the alibis. His parents had returned to retrieve his belongings and to talk to the Dean about their son.

"I guess he was just so devastated by the horror of arson and murder that he doesn't want to relive any memories of it," Mrs. Collins had remarked to Dean Atkins.

Lou wanted to talk to Don. Don and his parents, Steve and Mary, agreed to interviews so Lou made the long trip to Port Huron.

Lou checked into the Thomas Edison Inn north of downtown Port Huron around three o'clock in the afternoon. After he unpacked, he drove to the Collins' home, a palatial estate on the St. Clair River. At the top of the drive, a valet opened the driver's side door and assisted Lou before taking the car to a carport on the property.

At the door, the butler greeted Lou and announced his arrival to a maid, who led Lou into the den where he shook hands with Steve and Mary Collins, and was introduced to Don.

"Thank you for meeting with me," Lou began.

"You're welcome. Refreshments will be ready soon. Did you have a pleasant trip?" Mary asked.

"Long, but pleasant, yes, thank you."

"We must be pretty important to your investigation for you to travel across the state to talk to us," Steve said.

"My work involves unraveling the recent past, and I need to talk to as many people as possible. So, yes, you are important to my investigation."

Don was obviously nervous. He couldn't seem to get comfortable in his chair and rarely made eye contact with Lou.

"You must have some questions for us," Mary began.

"Yes, I do. Let me begin with a general question for Don: Do you have anything to say about the arson and murder at Alma? I have specific questions, but maybe you have something to share with me."

Don stared at the floor or to one side of Lou. He spoke softly in a monotone. "After the fire and the murder, the students in Chemistry

231 met and decided to make up stories about where they were during these crimes. I said I was going to tell the truth, which was that I went home."

"Why would they make up stories?" Lou asked.

"They wanted to make it very clear that they were not involved."

"But, were they involved, Don?"

"I'm not going to say anything more about that."

As Lou continued with a question, Steve went to a desk in the library and dialed a number. Lou couldn't attend to his discussion with Don while listening to Steve's phone conversation, but common sense told him Steve was calling the family attorney. Presently, Steve returned to his chair and said firmly, "Don, Mr. Ponstein suggests you not say another word to Mr. Searing until he arrives."

"Okay, Dad," Don responded.

Lou was not pleased. He finally had something substantial linking the students to the crimes, and now his source of information had been muzzled. The four waited uncomfortably in the Collins home for the next half-hour, during which time they exchanged some chit-chat about Michigan winters and some sports talk about the Detroit Lions.

When Mr. Jake Ponstein, the Collins' attorney arrived, he asked to speak privately with the family in another room. Lou took a crossword puzzle from his briefcase and did his best to figure out some of the trickier items. After another half-hour the four entered the den from the living room.

Mr. Ponstein began. "Mr. Searing, we are aware that you have come a long way to talk to the Collins family. We also hope the crimes at Alma College will soon be solved. But I believe it is in the best interests of my clients that we no longer discuss these matters. I trust you understand?"

"Of course, but you should all understand I'm only trying to help the college by investigating these crimes and finding the perpetrator. Your reluctance to talk to me is logical, but you're working against justice." Lou looked at Mr. Ponstein. "You can imagine your client's reticence plants seeds of doubt concerning Don's involvement, as well as that of Mr. and Mrs. Collins."

"That may be, but it's in the family's best interest to remain silent at this time," Mr. Ponstein stood firm.

"Done," Lou replied. "But I think you're making a mistake, Mr. Ponstein; a visit with me that helps solve these crimes could avoid several authorities pressing you and the Collins family for information."

Don suddenly stood. "Wait. Let me talk!" he exclaimed.

"Son, I really think…" Steve Collins interrupted.

"It's going to come out sooner or later, and I'd rather work with Mr. Searing, an alumnus of Alma who is a Christian, than people I don't know."

"Don, calm down! You don't understand. Trust me," the attorney begged.

Don left the den briefly and went into the kitchen. He returned as his parents escorted Lou to the front door. While shaking hands, Don slipped a small paper into Lou's hand.

Once Lou was in his car, he read the note, "Call me this evening after eight o'clock. I do want to talk to you." Lou smiled realizing his mission might have been a success after all. He would do as Don suggested. He drove back to the Thomas Edison Inn and enjoyed a delicious meal while watching freighters ply the waters of the St. Clair River.

FOURTEEN

Doug Wilson's chase crew was fairly certain their pilot had been murdered by Janet Reid's chase crew, and vice versa. It was Terry Felton, of Doug's support crew, who had the idea of getting the two groups together to share their grief and talk about circumstances surrounding their respective balloonists' deaths. Terry contacted Sam Smith, the leader of Reid's chase crew, and the third member, Jim White. They agreed to set up a meeting with Linda, Barry, and Pat in Kalamazoo, Michigan at the Air and Space Museum on Portage Avenue

The six crew members sat around a conference table, three from the Reid crew and three from the Wilson crew. Tension filled the air because each "side" was angry with the other; each side thought the other was responsible for the murder of their respective pilots.

Terry opened the meeting. "Sam and I, along with Linda Ross, thought it would be helpful for our two crews to meet and talk. To get right to the point, Sam, Jim, and I imagine you're thinking we had some part in Dr. Reid's murder. I can assure you we did not, and we were as shocked and saddened as you were."

"You're right," Linda replied. "I, for one, was certain you were behind Janet's murder. In fact, I still think you might be. Janet was Doug's chief competitor, and that competition was fierce. We know they respected each other's skill, but there was no love lost between them."

Terry nodded. "That's true, and that's why we all think the other crew is involved in the murders."

"It doesn't help that your crew violated the ballooning rules on at least one occasion, and the rules of etiquette more often," Linda countered.

"Only in the heat of the competition," Terry said.

"Whatever the heat, it happened, and a lot of folks were angry," Barry said.

"Janet told us more than once, 'If anything happens to me, chances are pretty good that Doug will be involved,'" Linda related angrily. "Janet must have had a reason, so when she died, we immediately pointed the finger at Doug, and indirectly at you three."

"Doug never said anything like that to me," Terry responded.

Jim shook his head. "We knew of the competition, and even got into it with you folks. After all, we were in a competitive event."

"You probably know a suspect has been identified in Janet's murder," Linda said.

"No, we hadn't heard that," Jim replied, glancing at his teammates.

"An Alma student has admitted to torching her office and to murdering her, but I don't know if she was arrested," Linda offered.

"Hadn't heard that," Sam said, surprised.

"That's what we hear," Pat True said. "But we know she didn't do it."

"How do you know?" Terry asked.

"A bomb blew up in the basket. We were with Janet in preparation for the event, and nobody was in the area. There was simply no way anyone, especially someone we didn't know, could have planted a bomb in the basket," Pat argued.

"In fact, the bomb in the basket is probably the biggest factor in our accusing you folks," Linda admitted. "Our balloons were prepared within thirty feet of each other. Whoever planted a bomb would have to know where to put it, and how to get it near the propane tank without drawing any attention to him or herself. Who could pull this off easier than people who know balloons and who work in the area?"

"I see your point, and you may continue to suspect that Terry, Jim, or I murdered your friend," Sam said firmly. "But we didn't, and we hope to prove our innocence. Conversely, it makes sense to us that one of you killed Doug. After all, if you believed we killed Janet, it would be logical for one of you to seek revenge."

There was an eerie silence in the room. "Well, did you?" Sam asked.

"If we did, we wouldn't admit it," Linda replied sulkily. "What kind of fools do you take us for?"

"Are you willing to state that you didn't?" Jim asked.

"Let's just say, we appreciate your getting us together to clear the air," Linda replied. "I hope we can meet again."

"Whoa! You won't say you didn't kill Doug or participate in his killing?" Sam asked.

"If it makes you happy, we did not," Linda replied grudgingly.

"I came to this meeting assuming you did not, but after the last thirty seconds I wonder if you were involved," Sam said disgustedly.

"Silence does not signify guilt," Linda said. "I have the option of commenting or not. I choose silence. You said you didn't kill Janet, but for all I know, you lied."

"Yes, you can keep quiet, but your silence speaks volumes," Jim said.

The Wilson chase crew rose and headed for the door without goodbyes. The Reid crew remained seated and watched them leave.

Lou called Don Collins after eight that evening from his hotel room. Don answered on the second ring.

"Hello, Mr. Searing."

"Hi, Don. Thanks for your note, and for your willingness to talk with me."

"I had to. I am not stupid. I know the attorney wants me to be quiet, because to talk means I'll get myself in a lot of trouble. But I really don't have a choice."

"You always have a choice," Lou said.

"Not this time. You can't hold my beliefs and keep quiet about what might explain a devastating fire and the murder of a faculty member."

"I respect that, Don. Why did you want me to call?" Lou asked.

"Following the murder, Dr. Reid's class met, and broke into groups to create alibis. Each group shared their alibi, and then Bert Dugan commented on the alibi."

"They needed alibis because they set the fire and killed Dr. Reid?" Lou asked, hoping for an affirmative answer that would wrap up the case.

"I don't know whether they did or not. All I know is that they didn't want what happened to those Duke lacrosse players to happen to them. If my classmates had substantiated alibis, they believed they would be in the clear."

"I see. So when I talk to them, I'll hear fabricated stories. Is that what you're saying?" Lou asked.

"Yes."

Lou asked. "I take it the truth lies beneath the false alibis?" Lou asked.

"I guess it does."

"What is the truth? Did the class plot to murder Dr. Reid?" Lou asked.

"Not as far as I know. It certainly wasn't a class project, if that's what you mean."

"Did someone kill her on behalf of the class?" Lou continued his questioning.

"I don't know."

"Did students set the fire or conspire as a group to set the fire?"

"I don't know," Don admitted.

"Did you set the fire, Don?"

Don took a deep breath. "I got a call from Becky Mulligan's father asking me to do it. He said nobody would die; only an office would be burned, and he assured me that the college had insurance. So, he asked me to burn the office in hopes that the exams and grade sheet were still there."

"But, why did he call you?" Lou asked.

"I don't know for sure. I think he is a volunteer fireman, probably knows how to stage a fire that would appear to be an accident. If you fight them, I guess you would know how to set them."

"Does the rest of the class know?" Lou asked.

"I don't think so, unless Becky's father told her and she told the others. Mr. Mulligan said he would never reveal who set the fire."

"How do you explain Suzanne Starmann's admission that she set the fire?" Lou asked.

"The more publicity you get, the greater your chances for glory, right?" Don asked.

"I suppose so," Lou replied.

"It's why a book banned in Boston will likely sell more copies than a book not banned in Boston," Don replied. "Do you think the bad publicity about Hollywood stars won't bring them greater fame and money and opportunities? I don't. Not for a minute."

"So, Suzanne admitted setting the fire to draw attention to herself?" Lou concluded.

"I think so," Don said. "The students appreciate her taking the spotlight off them. She gets nationwide attention. Some true-crime writer will publish her story, or someone will make a movie."

"But if she's found guilty, she'll be in jail a long time," Lou added.

"Sure, every decision has consequences. You weigh the pros and cons, then act. I think that's what Suzanne did. She'll be the center of attention for months, if not years."

"What if she has a mental problem?" Lou hinted.

"Right. And I'm being recruited by the Detroit Lions," Don said with a chuckle. "Don't fall for that, Mr. Searing. More games are played on a college campus than you'll find in the Summer Olympics."

"So, did you set the fire?" Lou asked.

"I did not set the fire, although I was assured no one would get hurt, insurance would cover the cost and the professor would have a rude awakening."

"Well, apparently someone set it. Was it this Mr. Mulligan?"

"He called asking me to do it. I agreed, but I didn't act. Maybe he called someone else. I really don't know how the fire started. Maybe it was an accident."

Lou recalled the fire marshal's report. "That's a possibility. Now, how about the murder of Dr. Reid?"

"You mean, did I do it?" Don asked.

"Just asking."

"Please don't insult my intelligence, Mr. Searing. Starting a fire late at night on a quiet campus is one thing. Taking a life is another. No, I did not murder Dr. Reid, and I don't know who did."

"You said it was Bert who suggested the alibis?" Lou asked.

"Bert Dugan."

"Is he usually a leader?"

"Not really. But, he's the one who proposed it, and he seemed to take charge."

"Is that his personality, as you know him?" Lou asked.

"I don't know. Do you mean, is he the sophomore class president or a campus leader?"

"Yes."

"I don't think so, but I don't know him that well."

"Thank you for talking with me, Don. You've been very helpful."

Don seemed to reflect for a few seconds on what he had said. "Consequences. I'm ratting on my fellow students, but what they did was wrong. And they planned to interfere with the investigation of a major crime — two crimes, actually. The truth should be told, and now I've done that. Good evening, Mr. Searing. Good luck finding the murderer."

Lou closed his cell phone and pondered this latest development. He added Don's revelation to his mental file.

Lou was beginning to think both crimes involved Dr. Reid, but in two different settings, committed by two different groups of people. Perhaps Mr. Mulligan plotted with Don Collins to torch the office, but that was the extent of his action against Janet Reid. So, perhaps the motive for murder arose from something in the ballooning world. Since he had been concentrating on Alma students and parents, Lou decided to shift focus to the ballooning arena. Perhaps then the picture would become clear. And another element was still missing from the equation: he needed to check out former members of the Delta Sigma Rho sorority at Lake Superior State University.

Jack wanted to pursue allegations of wrongdoing on Dr. Reid's part concerning the debate team. In the end, he truly believed there would be no connection; but Lou had taught him to explore every avenue, for one never knows where an important fact might be found.

Jack decided to interview the captain of the Alma College debate team. He had Lou's blessing, although Lou thought the effort would be the proverbial wild goose chase.

Jack met Mike Maus, a junior at Alma, in the Van Dusen Center.

"Hello, Mike," Jack began. "I'm Jack Kelly. I'm assisting Lou Searing in the investigation of the fire and murder of Professor Reid."

"Yes, I know."

"I understand that Dr. Reid was not the most respected debate coach in the conference."

"Yes, that's probably true. But I really don't know about her interactions with other coaches."

"Why do you think she wasn't respected as a coach?" Jack asked.

"Last year our team was disqualified from the conference debate competition for ethical violations."

"Please explain."

"You could probably get the details from Dean Atkins, but in a nutshell, she forced us to make up quotes pertaining to questions for debate. So, we were using false arguments to win."

"Made-up quotes?" Jack asked.

"Yes, and we fabricated court cases to substantiate our position as well," Mike admitted.

"What was last year's question?" Jack asked.

"Should Congress enact laws to challenge decisions of the Supreme Court?"

"So you supported or refuted this proposition with fraudulent material."

"Correct."

"And you won matches?" Jack asked.

"Yes. We used convincing arguments, and our opponents had no material to rebut our statements."

"And no member of your team stood up to Dr. Reid?" Jack asked.

"We all did, but she was the coach and it was a graded activity," Mike explained. "She insisted we do it. We probably should have blown the whistle on her, but we kept quiet."

"That's interesting."

"One member quit, but the rest of us went along with it. She assured us there was skill in defeating the other team and we were learning techniques of debate, so it didn't matter what material we used."

"You knew what you were doing was not fair?"

"Oh, yes."

"How did the cheating come to light?" Jack asked.

"The coach from Albion recorded our match with his school. He transcribed the match, then researched our quotes and references. When he found that we were making up material, he called Dr. Reid's bluff and that ended that."

"That ended what?" Jack asked.

"All our matches were forfeited. Dr. Reid was reprimanded and disciplined by the conference. But we were not happy."

"Why not?" Jack asked.

"In defending herself, she maintained that team members made up the material without her knowledge and had she known this, she would have handled it internally."

"That's a kick in the teeth," Jack replied.

"Yeah, we were pretty bummed out about it."

"What did you do?" Jack asked.

"We complained to the Dean."

"How did he respond?"

"Oh, he sort of defended Dr. Reid and suggested we stay on the team and if she offered any inappropriate guidance this year, we should tell him."

"How was this year?" Jack inquired.

"More of the same, but not as bad."

"Did you talk to the dean?"

"No. We decided it wouldn't do any good, because he obviously supported Dr. Reid. So, those of us willing to play along did so. We decided to compete, get our grades, and let it go."

"Sad, very sad. Did anyone on the debate team have anything to do with the fire or murder?"

"I can't imagine that, Mr. Kelly. Other than the cheating, no one had any reason to seek revenge. We all got As, and she even took us up for hot air balloon rides. We actually liked her; we just didn't respect her."

"I see. Thanks for talking with me, Mike."

Jack called Albion College and asked to speak to Dr. Chandler, faculty sponsor of the debate team.

"Dr. Chandler, this is Jack Kelly. I'm working with Lou Searing on the murder of Janet Reid. Do you have a few minutes to talk with me?"

"Yes."

"I've learned that Dr. Reid's debate team was forced to forfeit last year's debate matches because of cheating."

"Yes, that's true."

"And she claimed her team members acted alone in creating false material."

"Yes."

"In your opinion, was this true?" Jack asked.

"No."

"So she encouraged them to cheat?"

"That's right," Dr. Chandler replied. "But why are you talking to me?"

"Mr. Searing and I are trying to understand this woman, and it's no small chore. It seems that wherever she was involved, she had issues."

"Some people just have an affinity for stirring up problems wherever they are or whatever they do."

"What do you mean?" Jack asked.

"I'm not a doctor, so I don't know. Alma is a great institution, but they made a big mistake in bringing this woman to their campus. Evidently, they didn't do their homework in the hiring process. If they had, they would have noticed problems with her doctorate. Most debate coaches in our conference think her Ph.D was bought, not earned. Look at where she taught before Alma — Lake Superior State University — problems; then Alma — problems; her private life — hot air ballooning — problems. The list goes on and on."

"What were her problems in ballooning?" Jack asked.

"I have no specifics, but I hear from other debate coaches that rumors, gossip, or stories made the rounds. We all know that there's a kernel of truth in fiction. The woman was a sad case of not being comfortable with who she was. She needed to win every balloon event. She needed to win every debate match. She needed to be the tough and feared professor. She needed to hold a Ph.D. See the pattern?"

"Yes, I do."

"So, it appears someone decided to end the cycle," Dr. Chandler offered. "She went too far with someone."

"Any idea who?" Jack asked.

"Not really. You've quite a cast to choose from, it seems to me."

"Any chance that someone in the debate community had reason to kill her?"

"Mr. Kelly, please don't ask such a ridiculous question. In the intellectual community, we 'kill' with our minds. We have ways of destroying without resorting to the immaturity of violence."

"Thank you for talking with me, Professor."

In his Grand Haven writing studio, Lou's cell phone rang. "Mr. Searing? Mike Pritchard. I want you to know the prosecutor has officially thrown out Suzanne Starmann's confession. Suzanne's psychiatrist apparently convinced him that her admissions were all part of her psychosis. Along with her conflicting information as to how the fire started on the campus, her mental confusion was convincing."

"It doesn't surprise me, Sheriff. But I'm still intrigued with this young woman," Lou said. "I recognize her mental problems, but maybe she really did it and is hiding behind this disorder."

"I don't understand," Sheriff Pritchard replied.

"Well, she knows she has this disorder. Maybe she set the fire and killed Reid, planning to use the mental-health angle to exempt herself. But, what if she did commit the crimes — not as a part of her delusional behavior, but as part of her normal mental functioning?"

"That's possible. You think of every angle, Lou."

"It's just a thought. The fact is, she remains free, and the case against her is closed. But she could still be guilty, acting in a sane way, doing insane things."

FIFTEEN

October 12

The autopsy on Janet Reid showed her cause of death to be multiple trauma from the propane tank explosion. She had no drugs in her system other than medication for high blood pressure. And because the death was a result of the explosion, attention needed to turn in that direction.

When Lou called the Michigan State Police and asked to speak with an expert in munitions, he was transferred to Sgt. Elliot Garb.

"Sergeant, this is Lou Searing."

"Yes, Mr. Searing. How can I help you?"

"You've probably heard that an Alma balloonist was killed in the explosion of the balloon's propane tank."

"Yes, I've heard about the case."

"How could such a tank explode?" Lou asked.

Sgt. Garb began, "It wouldn't take much energy to ignite the tank, but two variables must be present. The first is a flame, and the second is access to the fuel. The best way to effect both is with a small bomb. The bomb would open the tank and the burner flame would ignite the gas, leading to an explosion."

"Does it require a timed bomb?" Lou asked.

"A timer could work, but my take on this case is that the bomb was probably altitude-sensitive, not timed. A timer leaves too much to chance. An altitude-sensitive bomb ensures that the explosion occurs while the balloon is in the air."

"I've never heard of an altitude-sensitive bomb," Lou admitted.

"Yes, you can program a bomb to go off at any altitude."

"Interesting. How big would this bomb need to be?" Lou asked.

"It can be quite small. You only need to puncture the propane tank."

"And where would the bomb need to be placed?" Lou asked.

"The propane tanks are usually along the side of the wicker basket. The majority of space is used for pilot or passenger movement. So, all you'd need to do is wedge a small explosive device between the basket and a tank."

"And this could be done at any time?"

"What do you mean?" Sergeant Garb asked.

"I mean, could it be placed there long before a ballooning event, for example?"

"Oh, I see. Yes. Since it's an altitude-sensitive bomb, it could be placed in the basket at any time."

"That's very helpful. Thank you," Lou replied.

Lou called Jack. "I want to take another look at the video from the Balloon Festival in Battle Creek. Can you bring it down to Grand Haven?"

"Sure. What are you looking for in the video?" Jack asked.

"I still think that whoever you saw rise up from the basket while it was on its side is either the murderer or someone assisting in Dr. Reid's murder. I learned from a munitions expert at the Michigan State Police Laboratory that the explosion was probably caused by a small, altitude-sensitive device, which triggered one of the four propane tanks to explode. The expert says it only needed to be wedged between the basket and the tank. So the person you saw kneeling by or emerging from the basket could be our suspect."

"Very good, Lou. But I can safely say, you won't be able to tell whether it is a man or a woman."

"We'll see."

Before meeting with Jack, Lou called Bert Dugan.

"What do you need?" Bert asked.

"I've called to have a father-to-son talk, if you're agreeable."

"Of course. You sound like you think I need some advice."

"Yes, I think you do."

"I'm ready."

"I want you to understand a couple of things. I know you and your classmates have fabricated alibis concerning your whereabouts the night of the fire and the morning of Dr. Reid's murder. I know that you believed that telling these lies would stump me and the authorities so that class members wouldn't be suspected."

"I don't know what you are talking about," Bert replied defensively.

"Yes, you do, Bert. You just don't want to admit it. You have a choice here. You can convince your classmates to come clean about what really happened or you can face the consequences of perjury. I personally can offer no consequences, but as soon as one of you lies to a police officer, a judge, or a jury, you'll find a police record is far more damaging than a bad grade. Do I make myself clear?"

"I'm listening." Bert sounded cowed.

"I'm not asking you to respond now, but I assure you, I am not playing games. I know what you are up to, and I know who was behind the fire at Dow Science Center. Think about what I have said, talk to your classmates, and recognize that your individual decisions will follow you for a long time."

"Okay."

"I know the Duke lacrosse players told the truth. They endured a lot of frustration, but truth won out," Lou advised. "You think you can avoid what they went through by lying? My prediction is that, in this case, when the truth comes to light, unlike the Duke students, you will be facing a lot of misery. This is a chance to rethink your decision to lie. Are we on the same page?"

"We are."

"Okay. Good luck to you, Bert."

As Jack set up the video at the Searing home, he remarked to Lou, "I've got a question for you."

"Shoot."

"Why haven't we talked to Dean Atkins at Alma?"

"What do you mean 'talked'?" Lou asked, as if offended. "We've been in touch with him often. He's helped us in the investigation."

"True, but we haven't talked to him about Dr. Reid. We haven't asked, 'Why did you hire the woman?' We haven't asked, 'What did you do to discipline a professor who seemed so out-of-control'?"

"I suppose we should do that, Jack. You seem fairly certain we'll get some interesting answers."

"I don't know about interesting. But, you've taught me that it's important to talk to as many people as possible, people who have a reason to be players, bit or major, in the case."

"Good point. We'll call him as soon as we finish here," Lou offered.

Lou sat on the couch behind the coffee table and with coffee and a notepad before him. "Jack, I have two reasons to view this tape. We need to study the portion where this person rises from the area of the basket, but I also want to know whether the film can be analyzed to obtain details about this person."

"What kind of details?" Jack asked.

"Gender, identifying marks on body or clothing, age, facial features, hair color. Anything that would help us identify the person."

"Okay. Let's take a look at the clip."

As the image came up on the television screen, Lou mused, "I don't understand — Why isn't this in HD? Doesn't this company use the latest technology in their filming? Why is this clip fuzzy compared to what I see on my home theater?"

"I think the photo image they gave us is the best they can offer from the camera they used at the festival. Much of their video is digital and crystal-clear, but they told me the camera they used here was for atmosphere, background. That's why the video isn't state-of-the-art."

"Can they do something to improve it?"

"No. Once it is captured with this equipment, they can't present it in another medium."

Lou sighed. "Okay, let's take a good look." Lou's cell phone rang. "Sorry, I forgot to turn this off. I'll only be a second."

"Hi, Lou, Maggie here. I've been researching Obsessive Compulsive Disorder." Lou's heart sank. He didn't want to tell Maggie the details were no longer needed; the prosecutor did not believe the young woman committed the crime, but that her comments were a result of her mental health, or lack thereof.

An idea struck. "Great. Maggie, Jack and I are in Grand Haven studying the video of the balloon festival documentary. Can I call you back in about an hour?"

"Yes. Sorry to interrupt," Maggie said.

"No problem. I want to hear what you have to say."

"I'll wait for your call," Maggie replied. "Good luck with the video, Lou."

"Thanks, Maggie," Lou said. He punched a button on the face of the phone. "Okay, my cell phone is off, so let's see the clip."

The video appeared on the screen. Lou and Jack looked at it carefully, playing it over and over, so they could concentrate on the single figure without needing to watch the entire footage in every viewing.

"What do you think, Jack? Is the person male or female?" Lou asked.

"I don't know. Could be either."

"This is what I meant about using other technology to find details the eye can't detect."

"For instance?" Jack asked.

"Could a tech blow up the feet and legs, to tell if the person is wearing women's or men's shoes? Can technology show shadows or color changes because of undergarments, for example? We can't see it, but if someone were able to blow up the photos, things might be visible that we can't see."

"I understand now," Jack said. "Yes, that might be possible. We can't do it here, but a crime lab — the FBI, or maybe a state police laboratory — could probably find images beyond the capability of the human eye."

"I'd like to know how tall the person is, for example," Lou said. "I want to know if any facial feature can be seen and the length of the hair. Can the exact spot where this person knelt be identified?"

"Yes, probably," Jack replied. "But why, though?"

"We might find something there," Lou replied. "A pen might have fallen out of his or her pocket. Who knows what we might find?"

"Lou, it's been days since the murder," Jack said.

"We need to look at the exact spot where this person was kneeling or sitting or doing who-knows-what." Lou thought for a second. "I guess you're right. We've enough going for us that we don't need to go over the grounds."

After viewing the clip several times, Lou and Jack still were not able to identify the person even as to gender. Finally, they decided to send the clip to the Michigan State Police crime lab for analysis.

With the projector off and fresh coffee in their cups, Lou said, "Whoever that is, I'm convinced that person planted the bomb in the basket, killing Dr. Reid."

"I don't think we can rush this," Jack replied. "That could be the balloonmeister checking each basket. That could be a member of the chase crew, or a crew member for another pilot who was authorized to get something in the basket. It could be an inspector from the Federal Aviation Authority. Lots of people could have a legitimate reason to be near that basket."

"For now, I agree. But, I'm sure the technology exists to glean more from the film clip. We just need to ask the people skilled in this work."

While Jack packed up the video equipment, Lou dialed Maggie McMillan. "Can you talk now, or are you busy?"

"Hi, Lou. Yes, this is a good time. I wanted to let you know what Heather and I learned about Obsessive Compulsive Disorder."

"Go ahead. I can take notes."

"Well, you know the basics. In general, someone with this problem believes that something or someone exists, when in reality it doesn't, or it doesn't pertain to them."

"Yeah, I understand that."

"Heather and I looked for something to explain your suspect's behavior and Heather found it. In a medical text it stated: 'Often in the early stages of a diagnosis, or before a professional can say with certainty that a patient has OCD, the patient may engage in behavior that mimics the disorder to convince others, usually doctors, that a disorder exists. This can be done for purposes of fraud, federal or state subsidies, or simply to avoid facing an unpleasant future event.' The article contends that rarely, if ever, does someone with OCD involved in criminal activity use the diagnosis to commit crime. But to repeat, until diagnosed with OCD, a patient may mimic OCD symptoms to commit a crime."

"Slow down a second, I'm taking notes… Okay, go ahead."

"The next sentence struck a chord with us. 'Often the person with OCD is overcome with guilt. The patient may admit to committing crimes or causing accidents, and often seeks out police, clergy, or family members of victims to apologize and seek forgiveness."

"Again, wait a second. I'm writing… Okay, any more?"

"No, that's it. Heather and I think that this coed probably does have OCD, as the psychiatrist stated. But if she is a borderline case, or if the physician is wrong in his diagnosis, she may see an opportunity to feign OCD to be a hero in a sense. Not only is she freeing her friends of this perceivably evil woman, but she also can become a martyr, suffering so that others can enjoy a benefit. In this case, the benefit is freedom from this woman and the evil that she appears to bring to her students."

"Interesting. So, if a judge throws out this person's admission because of a mental health disorder, you're saying she might be feigning the disorder to be a hero. And, in fact, could have committed the crimes."

"That's possible, Lou. I'm not suggesting you wrap up the case, but I'd take this coed's confession seriously."

"Well, in Suzanne Starmann's confession she describes torching Reid's office on Alma's campus, but her description is not what the fire marshal says started the fire. Another student has also admitted to knowing of plans to set the fire, and it was an adult who offered advice for his crime. In neither instance is Suzanne mentioned."

"Interesting. Maybe this Suzanne really had nothing to do with it, Lou. What Heather and I are suggesting is that she might be playing both ends against the middle. She may be the criminal, but her means of committing the crimes is explained by the mental disorder, not the reality of how she did it."

"Okay, we'll chew on that, Maggie. Thank you, and please thank Heather for me. You two have been a great help."

"Glad to help, Lou."

"Thanks, Maggie. Talk with you soon."

Lou closed his cell phone and turned to Jack. "We asked her for help and we got it, but all it does is muddy the water."

"Is it time for you to call Dean Atkins?" Jack asked.

"Since we're both here and have the time, it would be a good idea."

Lou made the call, and the dean agreed to talk via Lou's speaker phone.

"Thanks for talking with us on short notice, Dean," Lou began.

"Are you any closer to solving these crimes?" John Atkins asked.

"We're always getting closer, and I'm not trying to be a smart aleck. We have several ideas and theories, so yes, we're getting there. But we have a lot of work to do before we can say, 'Case closed.'"

"How can I help you? As you can imagine, every day prolongs the discomfort on campus. And there are contingent problems — donations, applications for admission, faculty recruitment. An open case of faculty murder sends ripples a long way from the center of the crime."

"Yes, we can imagine."

"So, how can I help you?"

"Jack, you start," Lou directed.

"Dean, did you know of Janet Reid's dubious past, and if so, why did you recruit her for Alma?"

"I had heard a few things, but I didn't believe that what I learned would pose problems here."

"What, for example?" Jack followed up.

"For example, the sorority matter at Lake Superior State University. I knew that Dr. Reid didn't use good judgment in following protocol, but on the other hand, she took action when she knew of the drinking. I liked that — a faculty member having the courage to inform the administration about violation of policies. That's a strength, in my opinion. That she should have done so in a more appropriate manner is small potatoes. I thought we could work around that with counseling, if necessary."

"Had you heard of questions surrounding her doctorate?" Lou asked.

"Yes, that was hinted at in a letter of recommendation. That in itself was odd because letters of recommendation are always positive and rarely give you a realistic picture of an individual. One of the letters suggested we look into possible discrepancies."

"Did you?" Jack asked.

"I must say no. In retrospect, I should have, but we liked her in the interview. We liked her knowledge of chemistry, her interest in doing research and in publishing. We liked her high standards and her willingness to participate in student activities, like the debate team. We accepted her letters of recommendation, glowing as they were. I guess we decided, with all those accolades, she must truly have earned her degree."

"After she was hired, did you learn anything more?" Lou wondered.

"Yes, I did." Dean Atkins paused. "It turns out she didn't actually complete her degree. She had been enrolled in a doctoral program, but she didn't finish the dissertation. She was actually ABD — all but dissertation — but she decided to give herself the degree anyway. She put it on her vita and was hired at Lake Superior State University. I guess we were buffaloed as well."

"Did you have any clue to her personality prior to her hiring, any idea of her need to win at all costs? I mean like her cheating in debate matches?" Jack asked.

"None other than that, as faculty sponsor for the sorority at Lake Superior State, she had no other experience with students outside of the classroom. And last year's debate-team scandal wasn't good for Alma's reputation."

"No, I imagine it wasn't," Lou admitted.

"President Shanks sent a firm letter of apology to the presidents of the schools affected. Again, I believed Janet when she said the students were responsible for the cheating. She claimed she didn't know of it and that it arose from the overwhelming desire of her team members to win."

"You've since learned that she was behind the cheating?" Jack asked.

"Yes."

"So you now know she was lying to you."

"Yes."

"The students — did they come to you with complaints?" Lou asked.

"Oh my, yes. I must have had four or five a week. At first I thought they were kids who just couldn't handle the tough standards, but after a while, I saw a pattern."

"And you didn't like the pattern," Lou predicted.

"No, I most certainly did not."

"Did you hear from parents?" Jack asked.

"Mr. Kelly, there were days when I dreaded coming to work, for I could hardly face another call from a parent. Parents can be mean and they were. On the one hand, I don't blame them; they and their children are our consumers, our bread and butter. But on the other hand, every student has been entrusted to us for an education. Dr. Reid was teaching material included in the curriculum, and, as far as the science department chair and I were concerned, the students were learning what we believe they need for a good liberal arts education."

Lou took over the questioning. "So, it sounds like Dr. Reid was becoming a problem."

"Yes, the concerns seemed to be multiplying."

"I'm curious whether you consulted with the president about letting this woman go?" Jack asked.

"Yes, I did, but in doing so I learned that Dr. Reid and the president were friends socially, and the president liked Janet, thought highly of her. Dr. Shanks actually hinted to me that she thought Dr. Reid might be dean material, and perhaps she should be groomed for my job, once retirement was in my future."

"I'll bet you loved hearing that," Lou remarked, shaking his head.

"My blood pressure went up a bit, yes," Dean Atkins admitted.

"So even though she was not tenured, putting her off campus was not an alternative."

"That's right."

Lou continued, "Dean Atkins, when you learned of the murder, what was your reaction?"

"I cried crocodile tears, Mr. Searing. My problem had gone away."

"I'll bet it had."

"Of course, I was saddened to see how it happened. No one advocates violence as a means to solve problems, but as strange as this may sound, it seemed justified when it came to Dr. Reid."

"Are things returning to normal in some ways?"

"Yes. We recently received an application from a young Ph.D from Yale for Dr. Reid's position. She appears to be a scholar and teacher, someone who will publish, and who seems to enjoy teaching. If she gets the job, I expect she'll be a real plus to Alma College."

"That's good," Lou replied. "Thank you for speaking with us, Dean."

"You're welcome."

"Before we go, we're curious; do you have a theory as to who may have killed Dr. Reid?" Lou asked.

"I've given it a lot of thought. I'm not a detective like you two, and I don't have the benefit of your resources, but I don't think a student killed Janet. If the fire marshal is mistaken, a student or students burned the office, but I don't have a clue, pun intended, as to who might have murdered her."

"If the students didn't murder her, who did?" Lou asked. "Maybe it was you?"

John Atkins laughed heartily. "I can see why you might think that because my problem went away when that bomb went off. But, my friends, I assure you that I did not kill Janet Reid. I have respect for life. I am a student of problem-solving, and that's why I am the dean. Do I mourn her death? No, but I am not your killer."

"Thanks again, Dean," Lou said. The three men brought the call to a close.

Lou returned his cell phone to his pocket. "What did you think of that exchange?"

"It was just one more interview."

"Meaning it was a waste of time?" hinted Lou.

"Practically. His answers were company-line. He was honest, which was refreshing, but I don't think we got anything helpful."

"Oh, yes, we did," Lou quickly replied.

"We did?"

"One remark puts him into the suspect file," Lou said.

"Glad you caught something. I missed it. What? Tell me."

"He said, 'when that bomb went off...' How did he know a bomb went off?" Lou asked.

"The news media said that, didn't they? I thought that was common knowledge."

"I've kept every news item I could find about these crimes, and none of them said, 'a bomb went off.' All I ever read was, 'The propane tank exploded.'"

"Good, Lou. You really are good."

"For a hearing-impaired man I do fairly well, don't I," Lou said, proud of his picking up what could become a major clue. "Life got a lot better for the dean once Dr. Reid was gone. Maybe — just maybe — we have our man, Jack."

SIXTEEN

Dayton Chief of Police Bill Upleger called Lou. "Got something down here, Lou."

"Great! We could use some movement in these cases."

"I think we've solved the murder of Doug Wilson."

"How's that?"

"We've found a pattern here. The motel clerk noticed the license plate number when a car abruptly left the motel lot. The clerk became suspicious when she couldn't find the vehicle description or plate number with her registered guests. We know of a guy who seems to research well-heeled men coming to a given area; then he identifies someone coming with him, usually a non-family member. He stakes out a motel where the mark is staying, and if the opportunity arises, kills him, plants the victim's blood in the second person's vehicle to throw off the investigation, and then goes off, taking a wallet with him."

"He kills for a wallet?" Lou asked. "He might as well have studied to be a pick-pocket. Jail time is considerably less."

"Lou, you know as well as anyone that we're not dealing with logical thinkers in the criminal world. It took a while to put it together, but this apparently has happened in at least two other

places — Orlando, Florida, and Lexington, Kentucky. The guy hasn't been caught yet, but we may end his string."

"You don't have him in custody, then?" Lou asked.

"Not yet. We have him in the rear-view mirror, so to speak, with good surveillance on him. Nobody else will be harmed, but we need to catch him in the act."

"How so?"

"When the target leaves the motel in the morning for breakfast, he'll meet a double, one of our officers, who will drive back to the motel and overpower the guy when he tries to attack."

"Since he travels throughout the country, how will you know where he is?"

"Oh, we have him in our gun-sights, Lou. We know where he is; we just need to be patient and wait for his next move. We've alerted police in Lexington and Orlando that we are on to this guy, and they're also waiting for his next set-up. We'll work with the police wherever he happens to be."

"This is great news," Lou said. "So, if you're right, Wilson's murder has no connection with Janet Reid's chase crew, or Reid's murder."

"Not at this point. We might find a connection, but I doubt it." Chief Upleger sounded confident.

"Thanks for the call, Chief. Looks like you're about to wrap up your case. Wish I could say the same."

"You'll get there, Lou. Yours is a bit more complicated."

"Please keep me in the loop," Lou asked.

"Will do, and you keep me informed, too."

Early Wednesday morning, October 13, the state police crime lab contacted Lou in Grand Haven and suggested that he and Jack come to Lansing. Lou and Jack were on the road within the hour. They signed in at the laboratory and were introduced to Sergeant Jerry Smith.

"I called because I wanted not only to tell you what I learned, but to show you," Sergeant Smith began.

"Fine with us. Any time Jack and I get to travel together gives us the opportunity to discuss the case."

"Good. First, the person could be a man, but my first thought, because of the earring, I tend to believe the person is a woman. She has her hair cut short, which is common enough these days."

"Can you come close on age?" Lou asked.

"I don't think the woman is as young as a teenager or even in her twenties or thirties. Notice how carefully she stands up, and she hesitates before walking away. I'll play the video now, and you focus on age and tell me what you think."

The video played upon a screen in Sergeant Smith's office. Lou and Jack watched carefully and could see the point. "Her rising does seem labored, I'll give you that," Lou remarked.

"Yes, someone younger would stand up quickly and then proceed. She's not elderly but not as springy as a younger woman would be."

"Ok, so we have an older woman with short hair. This is the kind of analysis I was hoping for."

"Now, look at her right hip as she stands with her back to the camera, about to walk away. Do you see what appears to be a round colored ball? It's small, but it looks like the red nose a clown would

use. You need to look closely, but in contrast to the background, you can tell it's in her pocket or attached to her belt in some way."

"Please play it again, Sergeant," Lou asked.

"There it is!" Jack said. "Why didn't we see that before?"

"But what is it?" Lou asked. "It certainly isn't a clown's nose."

"It could be a rabbit's foot on a key chain," Sergeant Smith guessed.

"Maybe, or it could be something on her belt," Jack replied.

"Yes," Lou countered, "but it's not likely. It wouldn't be part of a scarf. Is it part of a cap?"

Sergeant Smith adjusted the machine. "Let me zero in on her head. This will take a second. Hold that thought."

Jack and Lou marveled at the increased clarity of the picture. "Now here, see? The hair is pressed a bit. It's almost a moon-shaped depression from upper ear to upper ear. It could be a shadow, or part of her haircut, but it could also be hair flattened from a hat of some kind."

Then like a bolt of lightning, Jack spoke up. "It's a tam o'shanter! You know, that round Scottish hat — with the toorie."

"The what?" Lou asked.

"A toorie! That's the small pompom in the center of a tam. I'll bet she has a tam jammed into her pocket, and that reddish blob on the right side is the toorie."

"Well, if it is, there may be an Alma connection, given the College's Scottish tradition. The problem is we have no suspects who are middle-aged women with an Alma connection."

"We do now," Jack replied, writing on his notepad.

"Anything else catch your eye, Sergeant?"

"One more thing. Look closely at the left earlobe as I move in close. See that small shadow?"

"Yes. I can hardly see it, but I see something," Lou replied.

"That's a pierced ear without an earring in it."

"Interesting, but not unusual for a woman," Lou replied.

"I agree, but now I'll zero in on the right earlobe, and you tell me what you see." Both men squinted at the screen.

"Nothing," Jack offered.

"Wrong. Look closely. I'll move in slowly, and you just concentrate on the right ear lobe. Here we go."

Lou and Jack felt as if they were really seeking the elusive needle in a haystack. Neither man recognized anything. "You've got me, Sergeant," Lou replied. "Looks about as normal as can be. What are we supposed to see?"

"I don't see anything," Jack said, puzzled.

Sergeant Smith pointed. "It looks to me like the right earlobe has had some plastic surgery, probably after a tear. Maybe a child pulled hard on a dangling earring and caused a tear."

"Give me a break!" Lou said in amazement. "How can you tell that? I've never even heard of a tear in an earlobe."

Sergeant Smith moved to a computer next to the screen. "Here, I'll pull it up on the Internet — you simply type in 'earlobe' and you'll be surprised at the material you'll have at your fingertips. You can even find out about plastic surgery for earlobes. After the surgery, it's very hard to tell it has been done."

"I guess so," Jack said shaking his head.

"You see, an earlobe is simply skin and fat. There's no cartilage, so torn earlobes are common, and surgeons can repair them."

"How did you know to look for that, Sergeant?"

"That's why they pay me the big bucks, Lou."

"Actually, it's routine. In any analysis of skin area, we look for signs of possible surgeries."

"So, if we find an older woman with short hair who wears a tam, and who recently had plastic surgery on her right earlobe, we might solve the murder of Janet Reid?" Lou reasoned.

"Sounds easy enough to me," Sergeant Smith concluded.

"Well, we're off to do it then. Thank you, Sergeant," Lou said, shaking the sergeant's hand. "C'mon Jack, we've got work to do."

Once Lou reached home he discovered a fax from Dean Atkins. It read, "Lou, while reflecting on our conversation, it dawned on me that you might think it odd that I knew that a bomb caused Reid's balloon to explode. I learned this from President Shanks. Sheriff Pritchard had told her about the bomb during a routine briefing. I'm beginning to see things through your eyes and if I were you, I'd be wondering how I knew about the bomb, since the media have only mentioned the explosion. Am I paranoid? Probably, but in case you're keeping me on your list of suspects, this information might prove helpful."

After reading the fax, Lou called Mike Pritchard in Calhoun County to report what he had learned at the Michigan State Police Lab. Sheriff Pritchard's response was: "If nothing else, we'll now have security systems being placed at hot air balloon festivals."

"That's sad, in a way," Lou responded. "Now people can't simply go to a balloon festival without dealing with cameras, scanners, and who knows what other kinds of surveillance."

"Sign of the times. Two famous balloonists being killed, one at an internationally-known festival will do that."

"Unless something really odd happens, I think we're fairly close to wrapping this up," Lou predicted. "Jack and I are beginning to think that a parent simply lost it and took it upon him or herself to avenge wrong. If we're right, it is not the lives of the students that will be turned on end, but the parent's own."

"There must be a lesson in all of this," Sheriff Pritchard said.

"There is — Pratipaksha Bhavana. My yoga teacher told me about it."

"Yoga? You take yoga, Lou?"

"Absolutely. Yoga has done more for my mental health than any other single activity — except maybe when I was running races a couple of decades ago."

"But what does that term mean?"

"Pratipaksha Bhavana means that, when you encounter a situation that is not loving, is full of stress, or is bothersome; you simply escape and seek the peace that is within you."

"Some of us can't walk away, Lou," Sheriff Pritchard said.

"I didn't say that right, Sheriff. I meant to say, 'escape' attitudinally. You train your mind so that you can remain in the setting dealing with the negative, but your attitude can shift to the peaceful. Said another way, those who practice yoga have choices: rather than fight, argue, allow the situation to affect mind and body, we can avoid letting it have dominion over us by changing our attitudes. That is the lesson of this mess. If people who were upset with Dr. Reid had applied this practice, we probably wouldn't be looking into a fire and murder."

"But, they didn't."

"No, they sure didn't."

"Lou, you seem to put a lot of stock in this person in the video being a major suspect."

"Yes, I do."

"Who's to say she's not a part of the crew? Maybe she tripped and fell just before the camera caught her standing up from the basket. Maybe she's some innocent and logical person to be where she was."

"All of which could be the case; but I'm getting a still from the video to show various people because my gut tells me this woman is a person of great interest."

"I don't question your judgment, Lou. I just want to rule out the possibility that the woman is an innocent bystander."

"She may be just that, but I may up the ante because I think I hold some winning cards."

"We'll see — I hope you're right. I'll let you get back to your yoga."

"Thanks, Sheriff."

SEVENTEEN

When Jack had interviewed Mrs. Brigham, the housemother of the Delta Sigma Rho sorority, he had asked if group photos existed of the sisterhood within the past three years. If so, he asked that she send copies of them to Lou. A couple of days later, a 'Photo, Please do not Bend'-stamped envelope arrived at the Searing home in Grand Haven. The return address was Sault St. Marie, Michigan, so Lou suspected Jack's request had been honored.

Lou took the photos out of the envelope and glanced up and down the rows of coeds, looking for someone with short hair. He found a couple. One was obese, and the other was very tall: neither could be the figure in the video.

As he set the photos down, he realized that the housemother, Mrs. Brigham, on the far right in the first row, had short dark hair, and her body-build resembled that of the woman in the video. But the person in the video was not 83 years old. Lou concluded that the person on the field had no connection to Delta Sigma Rho sorority.

The next day, Thursday, October 14, Lou went through the mail that Carol had left on the island counter in their kitchen. Alma Accents, the quarterly college magazine, was half-way through the pile. Lou opened it and immediately turned to the Class of 1963 and 1964, looking for news about former classmates. Once that curiosity was satisfied, he looked through the rest of the periodical.

On Page 23, Lou found an article about the fire and murder, which he thought a bit odd. Wouldn't the editors want to suppress news of those events? While stories shouldn't be negative, people want to be informed, not suspect that information is being withheld. Apparently the administration and the editors favored candor. The events were presented in the form of a letter from the president, Elizabeth Shanks, to friends of Alma. It read:

Dear Friends of Alma College,

You may have heard about tragic events on our campus on October 2. A fire broke out in the Dow Science Center; and later that day, one of our professors, Janet Reid, was killed in a balloon accident at the Battle Creek Balloon Festival. We have cooperated with law enforcement officers charged with investigating both crimes. At this writing, the police believe there is a connection between the two events.

While the detectives feel they are making progress in the investigation, no charges have been brought in Professor Reid's murder. I have instructed our communications office to add a page to the college website so that those of you who are interested can be informed of the latest news. We will post only information approved by participating police agencies and our legal counsel.

The entire Alma family is devastated by these tragedies. Not only have we lost a valued professor, but our reputation has been tainted and we are feeling the negative consequences of these events. I ask for your patience, your prayers, and your support in days and months ahead as we heal.

Our students and faculty are safe. We are going about the business of educating our students. If any of you wish to talk to me about circumstances on our campus, I will be pleased to answer any questions you may have.

In the tradition of Alma, I am,

Dr. Elizabeth Shanks, President, Alma College

A photo of President and Mr. Shanks in her office accompanied the article. In the background on a credenza, a candid photo of the president and her husband caught Lou's attention. There appeared to be a strong resemblance between Mr. Shanks and the mystery 'lady' at the hot air festival in Battle Creek.

Lou called Dean Atkins. "Thanks for taking my call, Dean. First, I thank you for the fax and your explanation of how you learned a bomb caused the explosion. To be honest, I did wonder how you knew. My second reason for calling is an article in the Accents."

"How can I help?"

"When my copy of Alma Accents arrived in the mail today, I read the letter to Friends of Alma from President Elizabeth Shanks. It was a good decision to keep the college family in the loop."

"We talked about it at length and decided to risk more bad publicity by letting the readers know what we know." Dean Atkins sounded weary.

"A web page is also a good idea. I trust it was yours?"

"Yes, it was. I'll be curious to see how many hits it gets," Dean Atkins said. "But, you have a question?"

"Yes. At the end of the letter is a photo of President Shanks and in the background is a photo of her and Mr. Shanks, I presume?"

"That's your question? Who's with the president?"

"Yes."

"You are correct. The man is Gerald Shanks."

"I see. Could you arrange for me to meet him?" Lou asked.

"I don't think so, Lou. President Shanks protects him, and I don't know of anyone who has access to him."

"Does he belong to any service organization in Alma?"

"I think he is a member of Kiwanis. But, really Lou, I wouldn't want you to talk to him about the murder. I don't want the president to know that I pointed him out to you."

"Seriously, Dean Atkins, all I need is get a look at him."

"Why, Lou?"

"Can you keep something to yourself, even if it involves the investigation of the murder of Janet Reid?"

"I can if it doesn't compromise my morals or ethics."

"We have video taken by a documentary film crew at the Battle Creek Hot Air Balloon Festival. A person is seen getting up from beside the balloon basket as Janet and her crew laid out the envelope prior to inflating it. We only have a view of the person from the back, but the hair looks similar to the person in the photo with President Shanks. So, I'd like to see him and perhaps talk with him to see if he could be the person in the video."

"You're saying he could have murdered Janet Reid?" Dean Atkins asked sharply.

"No, I'm not. I'm trying to identify a person in a video, someone who may or may not have something to do with Janet's death. Until I see Mr. Shanks up close, or talk to him, I must consider him a suspect, and I'll have to report my thoughts to the authorities. If I can see him and rule him out as the person in the video, no comment need be made."

"You are suggesting that the husband of our president is a killer?" Dean Atkins asked, astonished at the accusation.

"Not at all. It's simply good detective work. I consider lots of people who could be involved. For any number of reasons, they may be eliminated or they may stay on the list. I have reason to think Mr. Shanks could be the person in the video and in order to drop him from my list, I need to assure myself that he is not that person."

"Give me a little time to see if I can work something out," Dean Atkins said.

"Twenty-four hours. But, here's an alternative. I need a close-up photo of the back of his head. If you can take that with a digital camera and send it to me electronically, I don't need to see him or talk to him."

"That might be something I can manage. I'll get back with you, Lou."

"Thank you, Dean."

Bert Dugan had considered Lou's advice and decided to call the Chemistry 231 students together once more.

"I talked with Mr. Searing," Bert began, "and I have asked you here today to tell you what I learned. Then we can talk about where we go from here. In a nutshell, Mr. Searing called my bluff. He knows we all made up stories so as not to be considered suspects. He knows Don Collins is possibly linked to the fire in Dow. He suggests that we clean up our act because if we don't, life will become much more complicated for us."

"Don set the fire?" Fran Henne asked. "I thought it was Suzanne!"

"I don't know that he set the fire. I understand he may have been involved. Let's not jump to conclusions."

"So, does Mr. Searing think we planned the fire?" Ted Skinner asked.

"I don't know," Bert admitted. "He didn't say as much, but he knows we were prepared to lie about our whereabouts. I think he knows about Mr. Mulligan's involvement, too."

"So, is Suzanne off the hook now?" Sherry asked.

"She took the attention off the rest of us," Bert replied, "so we owe her a debt of gratitude for her gutsy work. Her psychiatrist explained that she has Obsessive Compulsive Disorder. She only thinks she burned the building and killed Dr. Reid, and the prosecutor accepted that reasoning. Mr. Searing never believed she set the fire because of inconsistencies in her story."

"Inconsistencies?" Ted asked.

"Yeah. Remember, she said she poured gasoline under the office door? She wouldn't have known how Don set the fire, if he did set the fire."

"So what do we do now, Bert?" Anne Heron asked.

"That's what we need to decide," Bert replied.

"Does Mr. Searing consider us cleared concerning the murder?"

"He didn't mention the murder, so I'm not sure where his head is on that."

"Thank goodness he hasn't tied us to the murder."

"You've got that right," Bert said.

"I have to say, I feel terrible about what we've done and what has happened," Fran offered. "I think Dr. Reid really had our best interests at heart. She gave all of us good grades. She was just trying to toughen us up. Like a good coach, she was just putting our egos in their places and teaching us how to handle a little adversity. I think it's sad, what we've done to deceive people."

"Fran, relax, the college has insurance. No one was hurt. Yes, it was a crime and Don may pay dearly, as may Suzanne, but because of their actions we can get on with our lives."

"I will never forget this," Fran replied. "Most graduates remember turning the pews around in the chapel or maybe a bit of hazing. But we'll all recall the destruction on our beautiful campus and the killing of a professor."

"Just ,remember — we didn't kill her!" Bert Dugan reminded them.

Of all the students in Dr. Reid's class, Al Nowak was the one most affected by the mid-term exam grade. When Dean Atkins mentioned that counseling was available, Al took advantage of the opportunity for help.

Al had come to Alma from Munising, Michigan. He was an above-average student who scored very high on college entrance examinations, but he was an immature young man, not in his behavior, but in his manner of thinking. Dr. Reid's grade and lecture devastated him. His goal at Alma was to prepare for the Presbyterian ministry following in the footsteps of his Grandfather Nowak, who had been his mentor all his life.

Al was popular on campus and he had been recruited to join the Tau Kappa Epsilon fraternity. His grandfather advised against his joining a fraternity so soon in his college career, but Al craved the attention of his peers.

Each pledge was assigned a "father," an active member who guided him through the pledge period. This mentor was responsible to see that the pledge remained in good standing academically. In a sense, the mentor stood in for the pledge's father. Al became quite close to his "father," Bill Dillon.

A senior, Bill was a member of the track team and since this was the fall, he was on the cross-country team. Between vigorous training and very long runs, Bill spent most of his waking hours studying, going to class, and working out. What free time he had he devoted to Al, listening, giving advice, and helping him adjust to sophomore life at a demanding college.

EIGHTEEN

October 15

Dean Atkins put his camera in his pocket and set out to find Mr. Shanks, having no idea how he would get a close-up of the back of the man's head. If anyone saw him trying, the reaction would either be humorous or cause rumors and a questioning of his motives. The dean knew sometimes Mr. Shanks accompanied his wife to Chapel so he planned to sit behind the couple to take the photo. But the opportunity didn't present itself during the campus chapel service.

Following the service, Dean Atkins sat in a booth at the student center with Dr. Leonard Zwick, a member of the chemistry faculty. He ordered a Coke and took out his camera, pretending to be changing a battery or checking whether the batteries were in the camera. Coincidentally, Professor Zwick's hairstyle was similar to Mr. Shanks', short and dark, and the two men were close in age, by Dean Atkins' reckoning.

While the two were talking, Leonard began a casual conversation with Professor Phillipi who was sitting in a booth behind Dean Atkins. So that the two men could be more comfortable, Dean Atkins suggested Professor Phillipi take his seat since he was leaving. During the switch, Dean Atkins slipped into the booth behind Dr. Zwick and without the flash, snapped a photo of the back of the professor's head.

This isn't the back of Mr. Shanks' head, but it's close, and who cares, he thought. It satisfies Lou's request and avoids a meeting between Lou and Mr. Shanks. And more importantly, there is now no possibility of my being caught doing something so incongruous as taking a photo of the back of the president's husband's head!

Dean Atkins returned to his office, put the photo disk into his computer and sent it off to Lou with a short message: "Hope this helps, for it wasn't easy."

Lou responded with a "Thank you," and then forwarded the photo to the state police crime lab along with an electronic copy of the Accent letter and photo of President and Mr. Shanks. These materials were accompanied with the following note: "Sergeant Jerry Smith, please compare the attached photo of Mr. Shank's head (back view) to the video image from the festival to see whether they match. Also, please assure me that the photo of Mr. Shanks' head, is the same person who is with the president in the picture on the credenza."

Earlier, Lou had asked Dean Atkins for access to records for the students in Dr. Reid's class. The dean's hesitation was related to confidentially, but that was overshadowed by his wish to cooperate with Lou and Jack, so he relented.

"You realize you have no right to see the student records," he told Lou. "And, I know you're aware of that. However, I want to cooperate. Since you think there might be something in those records that will help solve the crimes, I'm invoking what we call 'situational ethics', meaning the situation merits not following the rule. However, there are three conditions: first, you may only review the records in my office; second, you may not photocopy anything in the student files; third, if you are planning to take notes or take away a written record of what you found in the files, I need to approve it."

"Your conditions are reasonable, and we appreciate being allowed to examine the records," Lou responded.

"I'll ask my secretary to bring the records from the Registrar's office to my office for your review."

"May we also see Suzanne Starmann's file, even though she is not on the roll for credit?"

"Yes. So there will be twelve student files?"

"Correct," Lou replied. "Thank you, Dean Atkins."

"You're welcome. We'll see you tomorrow."

The next day, Saturday, October 16, a home football game against Adrian brought visitors to campus. The day began cloudy and brisk, but football fans would call it a perfect day. President Shanks and Dean Atkins had campus responsibilities, but Lou and Jack were free to study the student records.

"Remind me, Lou. What am I looking for?" Jack asked.

"Anything that jumps out at you or strikes you as strange."

"That's specific! You can do better than that, Lou. Or maybe you could define 'strange.'"

"I'll look at the personal information first, then at the grades. I'll check any trouble the student may have had on campus."

"Trouble on campus?" Jack questioned. "They've only been here a couple of months."

"It takes more than two months to get in trouble?" Lou asked. "Besides these students must be sophomores since they are taking a 231-level class."

"I guess you're right."

"I expect to spend a little extra time looking at Bert Dugan's file and also Suzanne Starmann's. And, we're both going to look through all of them," Lou explained. "Two people looking increases the chance of spotting something significant."

The dean's secretary brought in a carafe of coffee and a box of muffins, and the two men set to work. While they studied student records without finding anything that could be helpful, Lou's cell phone rang.

"Mr. Searing? This is Sergeant Smith at the crime lab in Lansing. I don't think you need to come here, but I finished my analysis of the photos you sent."

"That was fast," Lou replied. "You work on a Saturday?"

"I do when you need information to solve a crime," Sergeant Smith replied.

"I appreciate it very much. Let me guess what you found: the person in the video and the husband of the president are a match, right?"

"No. The photos are of two different people."

"Really?" Lou asked.

"It's fairly obvious, Lou. Hair texture and color are different. And the biggest clue of all is, there is no pierced ear on the left side."

"Hmmm, that's strange."

"One more thing. The two people — by that I mean the man in the photo with the president and the photo you asked the dean to take — are also not the same person."

"Really?" Lou replied, a bit astonished.

"Really — we don't even need CSI to figure it out."

"We've got you, and you're better than CSI, Sergeant," Lou replied.

"Thanks, but I won't deceive you. No match, Lou."

"Thanks!" Lou passed along the information to Jack.

"Back to square one, I take it?" Jack said.

"Back to Dean Atkins."

"What for?" Jack asked.

"To ask him why he gave us a photo of someone other than Gerald Shanks."

Lou called Dean Atkins on his cell. With Alma winning 21-7, Dean Atkins agreed to leave the game and meet with them. After cool greetings were exchanged and the three had taken seats, Lou wasted no time getting to the point. "Why did you give me a photo of the back of the head of someone other than Mr. Shanks?"

For a few seconds Dean Atkins fidgeted in his red leather chair behind the cluttered desk, then sat up and faced them squarely. "Listen, I want to help you, but I can't take a picture of the back of our president's husband's head! I can't arrange interviews or chance meetings with the president's husband! I want this resolved, but I'm a dean of the college with a more than a full-time job. If you want a photo of the back of his head, ask the president, write a letter to her husband, or find someone to stalk him. I am not your third investigator!" Obviously, the stress was getting to John Atkins.

"You've made good points," Lou admitted. "We asked you to help because you're our contact at the college. But, you're right — we've pushed your buttons too often. However, having said that, I think you could have been honest with me and said no up front. Lying to me is about the worst thing you can do. All you've done is tell me indirectly that Mr. Shanks is still a murder suspect. What you did protects the murderer. Do you see our side of this?"

"Yes, I do," Dean Atkins admitted. "I am sorry. I guess it's all landing on me — pressure from the president, from the Office of Planning, from Admissions, from the media, alumni, parents, and from the people I am truly expected to represent, the students. Then add pressure from you two to the mix. It's my job and I'm not running from it. I simply couldn't take a photo of the back of Mr. Shanks' head, but I wanted to do what you asked so the police wouldn't come barging in here with subpoenas. I just figured you wouldn't notice."

Lou shook his head. "Mr. Shanks remains a suspect. I will not inform the police at this time, and Jack and I will continue to work on the case. Mr. Shanks may become uninvolved in the investigation, and this discussion may be for naught. Or he may become a stronger suspect, and we'll have no choice but to act."

"That's fair. Thank you, Lou."

Jack researched who had been officers of Delta Sigma Rho sorority during of Janet Reid's tenure on the Lake Superior State campus. The former sorority president, Barb Pope lived in Atlanta, Georgia, and Jack was able to get her phone number. After checking with Lou, Jack gave her a call.

"I'm trying to reach Ms. Barb Pope. Do I have the right number?"

"Yes, this is Barb."

"Ms. Pope, this is Jack Kelly from Michigan. Are you aware of the death of Dr. Janet Reid?"

"Yes. She was killed in a balloon accident, right? She may have been murdered as I understand it."

"Yes, that's correct. I'm working with Lou Searing, investigating the murder."

"How can I help?"

"Mr. Searing and I are talking with people who knew Dr. Reid and we understand that she was your sorority advisor at Lake Superior State University. We also learned that she reported some infraction of law or Greek policy to the school newspaper and to the chairman of the board. Do you recall this?"

"Yes, definitely. That was a difficult time for our sorority, and for me personally."

"No doubt it was. I don't know how to approach this other than to be blunt, if I may."

"Let me save your breath. No member of Delta Sigma Rho was involved in Dr. Reid's murder."

"How about the housemother, Mrs. Brigham?" Jack asked.

"Mom Brigham was angry, but Mom has dealt with many people over a lot of years. I can assure you that Dr. Reid was just one in a parade of characters that comprise a career on a university campus. To think that Mom Brigham murdered Janet Reid borders on lunacy."

"You sound pretty sure of that," Jack said.

"Mom Brigham was the one who got Dr. Reid fired!"

"I wasn't aware she was fired," Jack replied.

"Oh yes! Mom Brigham stepped up in our defense. She convinced the administration that Dr. Reid was not the kind of person who should be interacting with students on a university campus. She went toe-to-toe with Dr. Reid, her attorney, and the lawyer representing the faculty. And, what's more, she used the situation to teach us a valuable lesson."

"What was that?" Jack asked.

"I still vividly remember her calling all of us together and speaking for at least a half hour. She told us we would encounter trying and frustrating people and situations in our lives, and that the way to handle them was to remain calm, use our heads, and seek counsel from people skilled in problem-solving. You know, like ministers, mediators, counselors. We hung on her every word."

"I wonder why Alma College didn't know about this when they hired her?" Jack asked.

"You mean her firing?" Barb asked. "I understood it was part of the confidentially agreement between Dr. Reid's attorney and the University."

"You mean, 'Leave now, and nothing will be written into the personnel file'?"

"Yes. Her attorney insisted on that provision in the agreement so Dr. Reid could seek other employment."

"You've been very helpful, Barb," Jack said. "Thank you."

"Glad I could help. Good luck with your investigation."

"Thank you."

Jack felt comfortable in telling Lou that, as far as he was concerned, Delta Sigma Rho sorority and their housemother, Cece Brigham, had had nothing to do with the murder of Janet Reid.

NINETEEN

October 17

As is often the case in investigations, something bizarre and unexpected occurred. Lou received a call from the Alma Police Chief John Worthington.

"There's been another incident involving Alma College."

"What now? I'm almost afraid to ask," Lou responded.

"In addition to the fire, we could now have an attempted murder."

"Oh, my goodness! Who?"

"Dean Atkins."

"Is he okay?" Lou asked, most concerned.

"He'll survive, but he's one lucky man."

"What happened?"

"He was returning from a meeting in Lansing when he was run off US-127 into a wooded area between Ithaca and Alma. According to a witness, a car came along beside him and bumped him a couple of times. Dean Atkins sped up to get away from him, and the other driver also accelerated, bumping him harder as they approached an overpass. Dean Atkins left the highway trying to keep his car under control and hit a pretty good-sized tree."

"Any suspects? Could Dean Atkins identify the person who did this to him?" Lou asked.

Chief Worthington sounded weary. "We don't have any definite answers yet. We have lots of theories, but nothing points to any one person. We are looking for the other car — it should have silver paint from the dean's car on the passenger side."

By now, fear was the dominant emotion on the Alma College campus, with suspicion a close second. The Board of Trustees held an emergency conference call to discuss their proper response to the fire, murder of a faculty member, and an incident involving the Dean, which didn't appear to be an accident. Taking the lead, President Shanks met with the faculty, student groups, and community leaders; in each setting she provided calm reassurance that everything was under control. She explained that expert law enforcement personnel were responding to each situation and briefing her daily, more often if necessary. She convinced everyone by her demeanor and her words that the college was safe, that studies needed to proceed, and that events would soon be explained to everyone's satisfaction.

Dean Atkins underwent surgery following the accident for his extensive injuries. He'd lost a considerable amount of blood, and he had sustained thoracic injuries including a collapsed left lung. He was in intensive care from the moment he was admitted; he was allowed no visitors except for close family. The police expected he would be able to identify the driver, so they could wait to talk to him.

Lou and Jack made their way to Alma to learn about the automobile accident first-hand and talk with anyone who might provide an explanation for this latest development.

"I wonder if all of these 'troubles' are connected," Jack remarked.

"At the moment I can't be sure," Lou replied. "I think the fire and Janet Reid's death are connected. This latest development may or may not be."

"I'm beginning to feel sorry for Dean Atkins," Jack offered.

"Yes, the guy has a lot of baggage, hasn't he?" Lou replied. "By the way, the police have invited us to be present when they question Dean Atkins, once the doctors give permission."

Meanwhile, Lou and Jack were able to talk with Mrs. Atkins at the hospital in Alma. Lou asked, "Did the dean speak of anyone threatening him?"

"He's going through so much at the college," Mrs. Atkins said, shaking her head. "I've listened to his frustration over the fire and Janet's murder. You can't imagine how everyone has treated him — the attacks have been relentless! President Shanks should not have made my husband front man for this, but she couldn't have picked a better person. People feel a need to strike back, and they have."

"It looks that way, but did he speak of anyone threatening him directly?" Lou repeated.

"I don't recall that he was specifically threatened, but one person seemed to be on the verge of losing it so to speak."

"Who is that?"

"Bill Dillon, a student on campus. John said that on a number of occasions that he had almost called security to remove Bill from the administration building. I guess he complained relentlessly about what the college supposedly was doing to a pledge in his fraternity."

"Who was the pledge?" Lou asked. "Do you recall?"

"I think the boy's name was Al Nowak."

"And again, what was his issue with your husband?"

"Bill maintained the college was responsible for damaging Al mentally. He demanded the college find and pay for a psychiatrist to work with the boy. Bill likened what they did to Al to what happened to Dr. Reid, only he insisted the college was killing his friend mentally, and he demanded that John do something."

"I see."

"Of course, John told him he thought Bill was overreacting and that counseling was available. He explained that the college can't be responsible for every student's mental health."

"Okay, we'll speak to Bill Dillon. Could anyone else have wanted your husband dead?"

"I can't think of anyone. John said a lot of people were upset, but I don't recall a specific threat."

"Did your husband have any enemies, or as they say, skeletons in the closet as it were? Did he owe anyone a large sum of money? Did he have a drug problem? I ask these things presuming the answers will be 'No,' but I need to ask."

"The answer is 'No,' at least as far as I'm aware. We are private people with active lives, but I can't imagine John keeping anything like that from me."

"It happens all the time, Mrs. Atkins."

"I imagine. I suppose anything is possible, but as far as I know no one in John's life wanted him hurt, much less dead."

Following up on Bill Dillon's behavior, Jack stopped in at the Tau Kappa Epsilon house near the Alma campus. He could tell an active from a pledge because pledges always had to carry something, wear something, or in some way be identified as a pledge versus an active.

Jack spoke to the first active he saw. "May I speak to your president? Or actually, any officer will do."

"Our president is here somewhere, I'll see if I can find him. Come in, have a seat," the fraternity member said, motioning toward the living room which held a number of overstuffed chairs, all facing a huge-screen TV. The room was as neat as might be expected of living quarters for thirty young men. Jack heard the clanging of pool balls in the next room. On the walls were several photos of fraternity pledge classes. Jack looked for a photo in the early 1960s. The photo from 1961 had a subtitle, 'Largest pledge class in the history of Tau Kappa Epsilon, Delta Zeta Chapter.' Lou was there in the second row; he had hair, was fairly thin, and was fairly good-looking. Boy, oh, boy, time sure changes a person, Jack thought.

An active came into the room. "Are you looking for an officer?"

"Yes, I'm Jack Kelly, a friend of one of your brothers from the early 1960s."

"Oh, great, welcome. I'm Jim Greenlees, president of our fraternity." The two men shook hands.

"Who is your friend?" Jim asked.

"Lou Searing. Here he is," Jack said, pointing to the second row of the group photograph.

"Oh, yes, Mr. Searing. He's one of our supportive alumni. You'll find all of his books in our library downstairs. And you must be Mr. Kelly, the guy in The Lighthouse Murders. If I recall correctly, you're 'Groucho,' or something like that."

"That's me. But, he refers to me as 'Sancho,' his right-hand man."

"'The new Maggie' is how we refer to you around here."

"Well, yes, Maggie still helps Lou. In fact, she's been assisting us on this case."

"What brings you to the TKE house?" Jim asked. "Just stopping by to bring greetings from Mr. Searing?"

"That was one reason. I was also hoping to talk to Bill Dillon."

"You're out of luck. He's at work and won't be back till late tonight."

"Then do you know where I can find Doc Pattison?"

"Yes. Doc lives at Masonic Pathways on Wright Ave. I've got his number if you would like it."

Jack nodded. Jim wrote Doc's number on a notepad.

"Doc is our biggest supporter," Jim said, handing Jack the note.

"Lou speaks highly of him. He said if I ever needed information about TKE or its members, Doc would know. Is Doc still teaching English?" Jack asked. "Lou said he was a great professor."

"No, Doc retired a few years ago," Jim replied. "He holds the well-deserved title of Professor Emeritus. I never met a man more dedicated to his students."

"Thanks. Now if you'll give me directions to this Masonic Pathways, I'll be on my way."

"Sure. If you don't mind my asking, is Bill in some kind of trouble?" Jim asked.

"We just want to talk with him since his name came up in one of our interviews. We have a long list of people who might be able to help us."

"I see. Well, to get to Masonic Pathways, go north to Superior Street, turn right past the railroad tracks, and turn left on Wright Avenue. You can't miss the place on your right — it looks like a huge estate in Virginia — got a million windows. One of our pledge activities is to count the number of windows, and believe me, it can get ugly if a pledge misses the exact number."

Jack shrugged his shoulders. "Whatever. Thank you, Jim."

"Glad I could help. Our regards to frater Searing."

TWENTY

Jack Kelly found the Masonic Home on Wright Avenue. In the entry of the massive building, he asked the receptionist to page Doc Pattison. Within a couple of minutes, Doc appeared in the lobby.

"Doc Pattison?"

"Yes."

"I'm Jack Kelly. I'm working with Lou Searing, investigating the murder of Janet Reid."

"Nice to meet you, Mr. Kelly. Welcome to my new home." Doc extended his hand and Jack took it.

"Thanks."

"Have a seat. I'll ask for coffee if you'd like some."

"No thanks. I'm doing just fine."

"Listen, any friend of Lou's is a friend of mine. How can I help you?" Doc asked.

"I presume you have been following events at the college?"

"Yes. Terrible, just terrible. What is the world coming to?"

"Makes you wonder, doesn't it?" Jack replied shaking his head.

"Your being here means you think I can help you and Lou. I hope I can."

"I hope so too. We're trying to find out about a couple of TKEs, and you're the source when it comes to TKE information."

"I don't know about that, but tell me what you need to know."

"We are interested in two fraters, one sophomore, and one senior. They're Al Nowak and Bill Dillon."

"I guess if I had said, 'Wait, don't tell me,' I'd have guessed those two," Doc replied. "Well, what can I say? They're about as different as two young men can be and yet they seem to have bonded."

"We thought that might be the case."

"Let me start with Bill. He's intelligent, and an exceptional athlete. Bill knew Janet Reid, and in fact, he went ballooning with her for a few months."

"He's a pilot?" Jack asked.

"He wanted to become one, so Janet gave him some lessons, and for a brief period I think he was a member of the chase crew. But they had a falling-out over something, and that shared ballooning interest faded."

"This falling-out…" Jack began when Doc interrupted.

"I didn't hear all the details, but it wasn't anything of significance. In fact, I don't even remember it myself, but it was some minor disagreement."

"Okay, go on."

"I've talked to Bill more than once. I do know that helping a pledge was very important to him. In fact, joining the fraternity was important to him to start with. In our brotherhood, he found an acceptance that he never knew before. He was respected for his athletic skill and he took the Greek culture to heart."

"I understand he's on the track team." Jack said.

"That's a sad story. He was an all-conference distance man, ran like a deer and with as much grace. But he pulled a muscle at the beginning of cross-country season, and that has taken its toll. He became a bit depressed over it and his grades suffered. He got counseling and is on his way back to being his old self. His injury is healing, and his track coach expects him back in the spring, going at full speed."

"Anything else?"

"He's a physics major, pre-med, but between you and me, I don't think he'll get into medical school. He's too mentally unsteady for any admissions committee. Unless he has pull at some school, I can't imagine he'll be accepted, and if that happens, counseling had better be available because he will be devastated."

"Okay. Now what can you tell me about Al?"

"Nice kid, very sensitive kid. A good student, but I can tell you, that speech Dr. Reid supposedly made following the exam stunned this kid. He's never known anything but success, and he thrives on it. I heard that when Dr. Reid finished her diatribe and the kids left the classroom, Al contemplated suicide. Bill stayed with him and summoned a counselor on campus, but if Bill hadn't known what to do, another tragedy might well have occurred at Alma."

"Is the kid okay now?"

"I think so."

"Anything else?" Jack asked. "Any ideas that might help us?"

"I don't think so, Jack, but I will offer this: I'm very certain Alma is not connected with these crimes. I've been with the college for decades, and I can tell you that the students are the best, the faculty highly-respected in Michigan and around the country, if not through-out the world. If I may use an analogy, some virus has gotten into the Alma body and is wreaking havoc, but I will never believe that anyone connected with Alma set a fire on campus. And I am just as certain that the murder of Janet Reid has nothing to do with Alma, its students, parents, alumni, or faculty. When you and Lou resolve this, you'll find no wrong will have been done by the Alma family. And, you can take that to the bank!!"

"I hope you're right and I suspect you are," Jack replied.

"Please give my regards to Lou and ask him to stop out and see me when he has a moment."

"I'll do that Doc. Thanks for your time and thoughts."

Before heading home, Lou learned that Dean Atkins had been transferred to a hospital room from ICU. Lou contacted him on his cell phone and asked for permission to review Bill Dillon's records, thinking something there might be of interest. The dean agreed, and as Lou and Jack looked through the file, Lou spoke up.

"Well, I'll be. Now, this is a surprise."

"What have you found?" Jack asked.

"Here's a note: 'All tuition and fees for Bill Dillon are hereby paid through a contribution from an anonymous donor.' That's some gift. What's the story behind that?" Lou wondered aloud.

"Maybe he's being paid for knocking off Janet Reid. Is there a date on the note?"

"October 5."

"Well, that's after the murder. It bears looking into."

"I agree."

When Jack and Lou asked Dean Atkins about this write-off of college tuition, he directed them to Becca Norris, Director of the Advancement Office. Becca welcomed Lou and Jack, offering them seats in front of her walnut desk

Lou began, "Thank you for seeing us on such short notice."

"I hope I can be helpful," Becca replied. "And, I'm 'Becca,' please. It's short for Rebecca."

"Okay, thanks. Becca, Dean Atkins said you would be able to explain how Bill Dillon's tuition was paid."

"That's confidential, and even Mr. Dillon isn't aware of it yet, so I hesitate to answer you. Why do you want to know?"

"Bill Dillon is one suspect among many in the investigation of Dr. Reid's murder," Lou explained. "We've been following-up on the possibility that someone might have paid Dillon for committing this murder. If we find out who has paid his tuition, it would clear up that question."

"I understand. I can assure you that Mr. Dillon should not be a suspect. I ask that you keep this secret: Mr. Dillon's tuition was part of a hundred-thousand-dollar donation to Alma College from Mr. and Mrs. Nowak. They were impressed with the compassion this young man showed their son Al, doing what he could to support him in pledging the fraternity. They especially appreciated Bill's handling of the crisis that arose after Dr. Reid's exam and comments. Apparently Al seriously considered suicide and Bill steered him from that course of action and got him counseling. Al's parents feel they owe Bill a great debt of gratitude. When they discovered he owed the college a considerable amount of money, they wanted to pay off that debt while contributing to the college."

"Thank you for sharing that, Becca. I assure you, neither Jack nor I will pass this information on to anyone. There is one caveat however: I write a mystery novel following every case we solve, so, before any book goes to print, I will contact you again for permission to use the information."

"I understand. Thank you. My guess is you should also communicate with the Nowaks if you do ask permission."

"I will, now, we'll be on our way. Thank you, Becca."

"Before you go, I have a gift for you."

"A gift?"

"I expected I would meet you someday, Mr. Searing. I found this at a bookstore, thought of you, and bought it. I'm sorry, Mr. Kelly, I don't have anything for you. Please understand." Jack nodded, smiling.

Lou opened the attractively-wrapped box and brought out a tan T-shirt bearing the message, "Be careful, you could end up in my next novel!" The three enjoyed a hearty laugh.

"This is perfect!" exclaimed Lou.

"I'm glad you like it. Thanks for all you two are doing for Alma College!"

After parting handshakes, Lou and Jack headed for the hospital to pay Dean Atkins a visit. Lou and Jack went into the room not knowing what to expect, but they soon recognized a body cast with tubes and IVs hanging from poles near the bed. The dean's face brightened when he saw his visitors.

"Good to see you, Dean," Lou said. "Feeling better?"

"Yes, I am, thanks. They tell me it will be a while before I am back. Actually, this is the first time I've slowed down in months. Not the way I would have chosen to take a break from work, but it's what happened."

"Very frightening, what you went through," Jack said. "I'm glad you're recovering so well."

"Thanks. How's the investigation going? Have you wrapped it up yet?"

"Not quite. We've narrowed down our list of suspects, but we don't have enough to recommend anyone be arrested."

"Who's on that list?"

"I can't tell you that. It might compromise the investigation. I'm sure you understand."

"Yes. It was inappropriate of me to ask. I'm just anxious to get all of this behind us."

"I understand," Lou replied. "I do believe we'll wrap it up soon. Comparing it to a puzzle, I would say that we 'see' the pattern now, and we only need to finish filling in some sections of the picture."

"Do they know who forced me off the road?" Dean Atkins asked.

"I haven't heard. Did you get a look at him or her?"

"I don't recall the person's face, no."

A nurse appeared carrying a syringe and a small cup of pills. "Excuse me. I need to take my meds," Dean Atkins, said taking a deep breath. "I hate these things, but apparently, I need them to get back to my old self."

"I understand." Lou and Jack waited in the hall to give Dean Atkins a moment of privacy.

As the nurse left the room, Lou re-entered.

"Thank you for your help," Lou said, reaching down to shake the dean's hand. "Take care of yourself."

"Thanks, Lou. They say I'll be out of here in about a week. They just need to make sure no infection is making a home in this old body and that I have the energy to move around."

Lou contacted Bert Dugan by phone as Jack drove toward west Michigan.

"Hello, Bert?"

"Yes."

"Lou Searing here."

"Hi, Mr. Searing."

"Bert, Jack and I are about to conclude our investigation. We've found no evidence of students' involvement in the murder of Dr. Reid. But you convinced your fellow students to lie, and this isn't normal behavior. You can understand why I still think all of you may be involved in some plot."

"I guess now is the time to explain." Bert cleared his throat. "The evening after Dr. Reid's announcement, we arranged a meeting at the president's home. We demanded that President Shanks and Dean Atkins do something to right this injustice."

"I see."

"President Shanks said she would not take action. She told us that part of life was adjusting and adapting to adversity. High standards are one mark of a great college, and Alma College was fortunate to have a faculty member like Dr. Reid. By intervening, she would set a precedent whereby she would have to accommodate every disgruntled student or group of students. She told us to accept it and adjust to the situation."

"Not very supportive."

"No. However, Dean Atkins took the opposite approach. He was totally supportive, saying that treating young people in this manner runs counter to their becoming upstanding citizens. He said such behavior on the professor's part fostered mistrust and projected a negative image of higher education and Alma College. He pledged to do what he could to help us. So we were encouraged."

"What was President Shanks' response?"

"She just listened. She didn't say anything after that."

"But why did you lie, Bert?"

"My uncle asked me to do that, and he suggested that I be the leader. He said authorities might think we had killed Dr. Reid, but if the investigation got us into legal trouble, we could count on him to step in and protect us from arrests or trials. In return, we were not to tell anyone of his commitment to help us."

"But you're telling me. Why?"

"I trust you, Mr. Searing," Bert replied. "This has gone on long enough. A lot of people have been hurt, and we need to resolve the confusion. I know I'm betraying a trust to my uncle, and I'll bear the consequences."

"I admire you for telling me the truth, Bert. This speaks volumes about your character. You will have a fine career, whatever direction you decide to go."

"Thank you."

"Who is your uncle and where does he live?"

"Bernard Higgins, and he lives in Battle Creek."

"I'll do what I can to shield you and the students, but I can't promise you won't need to testify in court."

"I understand. I'm ready for that. The truth has to be told, and I already feel better about all of this."

"Thank you, Bert. If you need anything, just contact me, understand?"

"Yes, sir.

Lou briefed Jack about the conversation with Bert and then said, "I'm interested in Bert Dugan's uncle."

"Give me some time, and I'll have everything we need," Jack promised.

Once he reached Muskegon, Jack quickly got to work on the computer. Bernard Higgins was a banker in Battle Creek, and also a corporate sponsor for the Battle Creek Air Show and Balloon Festival. Jack called Bert and learned that Bernard hadn't played a large part in Bert's life, having married Bert's aunt only two years before.

While Jack was researching, Lou talked to Mr. Higgins on the phone. Lou heard over and over that Bernard claimed he had nothing to do with the murder of Janet Reid. He did admit to knowing about the failed exam and also that he was concerned for his nephew, knowing the students would be immediate suspects. But, Bernard had an alibi: he had been attending a Catholic retreat at a monastery in western Kentucky.

On a hunch, Lou called the corporate office of the Battle Creek Air Show and spoke to the director, John Ickes.

"Sorry to keep bothering you, sir, but…"

"Believe me, you're no bother, Lou. Anything we can do to help you is our pleasure.

"I appreciate that, John. I offer only one topic today."

"And that is?" John asked.

"Are your corporate sponsors given a pass into the lift area?"

"Yes, each corporate sponsor receives two passes onto the grounds."

"Are names associated with those passes?" Lou asked.

"No, we simply mail two passes to the corporate sponsor when we get a check. Who uses the passes is up to the sponsor."

"I see. Thanks for your help, John."

"Call any time, and if we can help, you know we will."

TWENTY-ONE

Lou called Maggie in Battle Creek. "I've another job for you and Heather."

"We're ready. Heather seems to think detectives are always in the middle of exciting action. I tell her investigation is mainly hard work, but she has this image, probably from television, that you are some glamorous character out living 'CSI: Miami.'"

"Oh, well, I guess she'll believe what she wants. Jack and I need more help, and since you live in Battle Creek, you and Heather can do more than advise us about mental-health terminology. I need to know about a man named Bernard Higgins, a banker in Battle Creek. His corporation is a sponsor of the Balloon Festival."

"Okay, we have our orders, and we'll report when we learn something."

Wasting no time, Maggie discovered that Mr. Higgins was involved with a new branch bank near Sturgis. His secretary offered that he spent most of his time on-site, supervising transformation of a competitor's building site to one of his own branches.

Maggie and Heather drove to Sturgis in Maggie's handicapper-accessible van.

"We may not be able to move around much there, Heather. Construction usually means dirt, mud, uneven terrain, and boards for walkways. We may need to interview Mr. Higgins in our van."

"But, the barrier-free rules sure help us most places, don't they?" Heather asked. She had gained a sincere appreciation of able-bodied mobility.

As Maggie pulled up to the construction site, Heather spotted a man wearing a brown suit and a yellow hardhat getting into a muddy pickup truck. "That must be Mr. Higgins."

"I would think so."

Maggie pulled inside the site fence, rolled down the window and shouted, "Mr. Higgins?" But there was too much noise in the construction area for her to be heard. Maggie then pulled the van into the open yard area and flashed the lights. A worker approached the man in the pickup, pointing toward the van.

The man in the suit got out of the truck and approached the van. "Hello. You folks lost?"

"No, we use wheelchairs and can't move through the area, but we're looking for a Bernard Higgins."

"I'm Bernard Higgins."

"I'm Maggie McMillan, and this is my friend, Heather Moore."

"Pleased to meet you." Bernard nodded. "How can I help you?"

"We're assisting Lou Searing and Jack Kelly in investigating the murder of Janet Reid, the balloon pilot who was killed at the festival."

"Terrible accident," Bernard replied, looking at the ground shaking his head.

"Yes, it was. We'd like to know if you saw anything at the festival that might help us. We understand you were a sponsor of the event."

"Yes, we have been a corporate sponsor since the festival began."

MURDER IN THIN AIR

"Could you meet us at a restaurant in town?" Maggie asked.

"Perhaps Mr. Searing didn't tell you, but he has already talked to me. I'm surprised he wants you to talk to me, too."

"Mr. Searing needs various facts and impressions when he works a case. If it's not an imposition, we would like to talk with you."

"Fine," Bernard replied. "How about the Savory? It is right in the center of town."

"That's great," Maggie replied.

"I need to talk to the construction foreman for a minute, and then I'll meet you."

"We appreciate it."

About a half-hour later, the three were seated at a table in the Savory restaurant. Maggie and Mr. Higgins had coffee before them, and Heather had ordered herbal tea.

"Again, how can I help you?" Mr. Higgins asked Maggie. "You wondered if I had seen anything that might help you and Mr. Searing."

"Yes. We're talking to several people involved in the festival."

"Well, I don't think I'll be of much help. We send a considerable amount of money to the festival, and in return we receive two admission badges for the lift area and four tickets to the event itself. I usually give them to people in my bank who are interested."

"Were you there yourself? Did you see anything that might help us?" Heather asked.

"No. As I told Mr. Searing, I was on my way to a retreat in Kentucky when the death occurred."

"I see. Can you tell us who received the lift-area passes?" Maggie asked. "Maybe one of them saw something."

"I told my vice president to give them to a couple of deserving people on staff. She knows who would enjoy them, so I don't know who received them. I didn't really need the passes because Eric Swanson would allow anyone into the festival lift area if my name was mentioned."

"Eric Swanson? Is he the festival director?" Maggie asked.

"No, he's the balloonmeister. He calls the shots related to the ballooning events. His job is to monitor activity in the lift area. Sometimes I tell friends if they want to get up close and personal with the pilots and balloons to seek out Eric and tell him they are friends of mine. He waves them in. Eric is one of the few people I know who can provide a favor that easily."

Maggie was about to ask another question when a gentleman approached the table. "Good morning, Bernard. Taking a break from your new bank construction? Ladies." He nodded at Maggie and Heather.

"You might say that. These ladies are Mrs. McMillan and Ms. Moore. Did I get your names right?"

"Yes, you did. Hello, nice to meet you." Maggie and Heather said, each politely shaking the hand of the stranger.

"This is Donald Sterns, the county building inspector," Bernard continued with the introductions. "I need to make him happy in many ways with our new branch bank. He's a tough guy to please."

"Actually, I'm putty in your hands, Bernard."

"One man's putty is another's rock, Donny."

"By the way, since you're here, I'll save a phone call or note," Mr. Sterns said giving full attention to Bernard. "You're approved to use explosives to shake loose the reinforcements of that old safe in the bank."

"Good. Thanks, Donny." Bernard turned to the women, "One more approval I need. It seems like I have to get permission for my men to use the Port-a-Jon. The world of regulations is convoluted."

"All to protect the public, Bernie — you know that," Mr. Sterns said, turning to leave. "I'll be on my way. Enjoy your day in Sturgis, ladies."

"Thank you." When Mr. Sterns was out of earshot Maggie continued, "Explosives? I thought they were only used to knock out mountainsides or to implode big buildings."

"That's a layman's notion, Mrs. McMillan. Explosives are really quite common in the building industry. One 'pop' often makes easy work of a difficult job when land, or in my case, a very heavy object, needs to be broken up."

"I see," Maggie replied. In her mind, Heather saw the balloon exploding at two thousand feet, but she showed great restraint by keeping her thoughts to herself.

"Do you have any connection to Alma College?" Heather asked.

"A couple, actually. My brother played football for Alma in the early 1970s. He was a gifted athlete and student. I also have a nephew who attends Alma."

"Oh, really? Who?" Maggie asked.

"Bert Dugan. Bert is my wife's sister's son. He, too, is an outstanding athlete and student."

"Great! That's a good combination for a young man," Maggie said.

"Yes, he's on the swimming team, their number-one diver. I go to most of the meets."

"It must be gratifying for you to see your nephew excel among his peers."

"Yes. He's sort of like a son to me, the son I never had. His father was killed in a motorcycle accident when Bert was four years old."

"I see. Was your nephew a student in Dr. Reid's chemistry class?"

"Yes, he was. I immediately drove to Alma to talk with Bert. I love the kid, and I needed to be sure he was okay. I could imagine his future fizzling right in front of him. I talked to the president about Professor Reid's behavior. She told me she supported the professor, talked about how much the college appreciated having her on campus teaching chemistry."

"Did your anger translate into action, Mr. Higgins?"

"Do you mean, did I kill her?" Bernard asked.

"Yes."

"In my heart I wanted to, yes. But, since Bert was resilient, I left Alma feeling like this was simply a bump in the road, and it would work out for the best. I wasn't even in the area when the balloon exploded. As I told Mr. Searing, I was on my way to a spiritual retreat in Kentucky."

"I see," Maggie replied. "What was your reaction when you learned that Dr. Reid had been murdered?"

"Of course, I was sorry, for a life lost is a tragedy."

"Did you suggest to Bert that he convince the chemistry students to create alibis to minimize the possibility that they might be suspects?"

"Yes, I did that," Higgins spoke softly.

"You did?" Maggie replied, surprised by this admission.

"I saw what happened at Duke when the lacrosse students told the truth. I reasoned that good alibis would remove Bert and his classmates from the list of suspects."

"But, if they were caught in lies?"

"I felt they wouldn't be caught. Not if the alibis could be substantiated."

The next day, Jack and Elaine came to Lou and Carol's home. With blue sky and Indian summer temperatures, the two men decided to go to Lou's favorite thinking ground on the Lake Michigan shore. They walked in bare feet, enjoying the sand that would soon be covered with snow and ice.

"Well, Jack. What do you make of all of this?"

"Quite a cast of characters, Lou."

"Sort of like The Lighthouse Murders, isn't it?" Lou asked. "Our killer could be any one of several people." He took a piece of driftwood and marked out a grid in the damp sand. Now, who could have murdered Janet Reid?"

"Shall we take turns identifying people?" Jack asked.

"That's as good a way as any. Go ahead."

"I'll begin with Bernard Higgins, the banker in Battle Creek."

"Good one," Lou replied. "I'll stay with the family category and write down Mike Mulligan. He was concerned enough about his daughter to advocate causing extensive damage to Alma's campus."

"I'll add Dean Atkins," Jack said. "He lied about the photo of Mr. Shanks. He had had it up to his eyeballs with Reid and all the problems she was causing."

"I agree. Or, it could be Bert Dugan."

"We haven't really discussed him," Jack added.

"He's a dark horse, the person who suggested the students lie. Why does anyone need lies, except to cover something up, right?"

"I guess so. Hmmm, I hadn't brought him into the equation. Okay, my turn," Jack perked up. "We might as well put down Suzanne Starmann."

"I thought she was history, Jack."

"She's in a category with Bert Dugan. There is simply too much going on with her; until we have this solved, I would like her on the list."

"Everyone is fair game. Let's see, it could be Don Collins," Lou said. "He may have set the fire, and while he denies involvement with the murder, he could be lying on the more serious crime."

"I'm at the end of my list," Jack admitted. "How about you, Lou?"

"I'll add Eric Swanson, the balloonmeister at the Battle Creek Festival. He was on the scene when the balloons lifted, and he was at odds with Janet over a book deal."

"Okay. Any more, Lou?"

"I was going to add Bill Dillon, but I don't think he's that closely involved."

"I was thinking the same thing," Jack replied.

"So, I guess the people we're putting aside would be the Wilson chase crew, the students, except for Bert, Don, and Suzanne, the Lake Superior State University sorority and the housemother, anyone connected with the debate team at Alma or any other school, and any parents," Lou summarized. "Oh, and Gerald Shanks, a very long shot, but he needs to be on this general list." Lou scratched out the list, and made a mental note to transfer the results of their beach discussion to his notebook.

"I can see why you and Carol enjoy strolling along this beach, Lou. It's peaceful and beautiful."

"Yes, each evening is special, Jack. We're blessed to have heaven right outside our back door."

Apple pie ala mode was waiting when Lou and Jack got back to the house. Carol and Elaine had prepared the perfect fall treat, coffee was brewing, and water was heating for Carol's tea.

The four sat on the all-weather porch overlooking the shore and enjoyed pie and ice cream and conversation about things other than who had killed Janet Reid. Lou and Carol described their trip to Germany, and Jack and Elaine raved about their train trip through the Rockies. Millie, the Searing's cat, rubbed against everyone's feet. All four, as well as the cat, were relaxed, watching the day draw to a close.

The couples were about to conclude their evening of vacation memories when there was a knock on the door. Lou looked at the clock and saw ten-twenty. Carol asked, "Are we expecting anyone?"

"Not that I know of. Carol, you and Elaine go to the basement — right now," Lou ordered. "Jack, cover me — go to the kitchen. Move."

"What's going on?" Carol asked. "Why all the fear when it could be Marie from next door wanting something."

"It could be one of our suspects looking for a confrontation," Jack replied, as he closed the basement door.

By now, Jack had taken his position in the kitchen, out of sight of the front door. Parting the window curtain, Lou saw two men on the front porch, neatly dressed but not in police uniform. He relaxed a bit and cracked the door leaving the chain engaged. "Yes?"

"Mr. Searing?"

"What do you want?" Lou asked.

"We are deputy sheriffs with the Ottawa County office. I'm James Northrup. This is Butch Cantrell. We have a message from Sheriff Pritchard."

"Let me see some identification," Lou said.

The two men presented their badges and IDs.

"Come on in," Lou said, releasing the chain and opening the door. "Can't be too careful, you know."

"We understand."

Jack had overheard the dialogue, and opened the basement door. "Carol and Elaine, come on up."

When everyone stood in the front hall, Lou said, "These are officers Northrup and Cantrell from the Ottawa County Sheriff's Department."

The six greeted one another. "I take it you haven't gotten a call from Sheriff Pritchard yet?" Officer Northrup asked.

"Not yet." Immediately after Lou spoke, the phone rang. "That's probably him right now." Lou put the phone on speaker. "Hi, Lou," Sheriff Pritchard's voice boomed. "You'll soon be visited by two deputies from the Ottawa County sheriff's office. I wanted to let you know that..."

"They're standing in the living room now, Sheriff. What's going on?"

"Guess I wasn't fast enough. Sorry. Anyway, I got an e-mail from an Alma student, a Bert Dugan, who said his uncle, Bernard Higgins has threatened you and Jack. We know where he lives, but our men didn't find him at home. I've got a LEIN bulletin out on him, so hopefully he will be pulled over somewhere between Battle Creek and your home. Jack could have a visitor in Muskegon soon, also."

"He and Elaine are here. So, we're to be held captive by these officers!"

"Lou, it's for your own protection. We believe this man is armed and dangerous and we can't locate him. Sit tight, and we'll get him. The e-mail could be an exaggeration and the guy may not be a threat after all, but I can't take that chance."

"I get threats all the time. What's different about this one?" Lou asked.

"This one is real — I suppose would be the best way to answer your question."

"Why Jack and me? We're small potatoes in the stew."

"You two are probably getting too close to solving the Reid murder."

"Sheriff, Jack and I appreciate your watching out for us, but I think we can do that for ourselves. Please tell these officers they can leave," Lou suggested.

"We'll accept your help, thank you," Carol interjected firmly. "Tell us what we should do, and we'll do it, Sheriff."

Lou didn't like losing control and he didn't feel he needed protection from anyone, much less a sheriff's department. But Carol was nervous, and to keep her comfortable, it was best to leave the officers in charge for the next several hours.

"Are we all staying here? Or can Jack and I go home?" Elaine asked.

"Since the four of you are together, it would be better for you to stay here," Officer Cantrell replied.

"I don't mean to disagree, but it would seem safer for us to split up," Lou offered. "I don't know what this man has in mind, but do you want both his targets in the same place?"

"Lou, for once, just do what these officers say," Carol said, exasperated. "They know their business."

"I know that; I just think..." Lou continued.

"Just this time, don't think! I mean, listen, and do as you're told," Carol replied sternly.

Jack asked, "What are you expecting? A bomb, arson, someone spraying the house with gunfire?"

"We don't know, so we'll be ready for anything."

Lou was still uncertain. "I really think you're taking this to extremes. Jack and I are perfectly capable of taking care of ourselves, and..."

Carol got Lou's attention with a glare, then raised her right hand to her mouth and drew her closed thumb and first finger across her lips, as if to say, 'Keep quiet!' Lou shook his head, but he realized that continuing to argue would get him nowhere.

Lou thanked Sheriff Pritchard for his well-intentioned help and hung up the phone.

Bernard Higgins was at his summer cabin on Sonoma Lake in Calhoun County, planning how to deal with Lou and Jack. He carefully loaded two hunting rifles with silencers into the trunk of a late-model sedan and then added several boxes of shells and a camouflage outfit. On the front passenger seat he had stacked Google Earth maps of the areas around the Searing and Kelly homes. Included were sketches of wooded and dune areas around Grand Haven, and a detailed sketch of the back of the Kelly house. Mapquest directions on a clipboard supplemented the Google maps of both residences. The vehicle had a full tank of gas and a radar detector to assure speeding would not be an issue during the trip to the Lake Michigan shore.

In Grand Haven, the deputies told both couples to go about their evening and to go to bed when they chose. Carol made up beds for her guests.

The officers called the four together during the 11:00 p.m. news. "This is our plan. Once Higgins' vehicle is identified on the move, he will be stopped and he most likely will be arrested. Meanwhile, the Grand Haven police department will provide backup, as will our department. We have officers in unmarked vehicles on main roads to Grand Haven. We also have officers in unmarked vehicles near your home in Muskegon, Mr. Kelly. Of course, our subject won't find you home, so if he goes there first, we'll track him to here, assuming he doesn't have a change of heart."

Again, Lou interrupted. "Wouldn't it be a lot simpler to send us to Traverse City for a couple of days of beautiful fall color? Why do you want us trapped in our home?"

With her eyes, Carol again communicated her lack of appreciation for Lou's suggestion.

"Because we want you covered," Officer Northrup replied sternly. "If you are 'out there', who knows what backup plan Higgins may have? Right now, someone could be watching this house and communicating directly with him."

"That makes sense to me," Carol replied, supporting the officers at every turn. Elaine appeared uncomfortable and tried to breathe deeply to stay calm. She turned to Jack. "When you talked about helping Lou with a case or two, I didn't imagine being caught up in a drama, certainly not a scenario in which you could be killed. I hope you thoroughly enjoyed helping Lou with this case because it is your last. Is that sinking in, Jack? This is your LAST!"

Jack wisely decided not to respond.

At 5:00 a.m. Lou came out of his bedroom to make coffee. Officer Cantrell was asleep in a comfortable chair, but Officer Northrup was wide awake.

As he returned from the kitchen, Lou asked, "Any action?"

"Nope. It's quiet. Suspect hasn't been apprehended yet and we haven't heard anything from anyone on the outskirts of Grand Haven or from Jack's neighborhood."

"He's not coming here, Officer," Lou advised.

"How do you know?"

"Just a gut feeling. I get them often and ninety-nine percent of the time, I'm right. We're only bit-players in this drama."

"Our job is to protect the four of you," the officer replied. "Decisions made around the rumored plan are not my concern. My only concern is your safety."

"Well, contrary to my ill-considered comments last evening, I do appreciate your efforts and I appreciate Sheriff Pritchard's concern for our safety as well. So, thank you." Officer Northrup nodded in reply.

"Did Carol ask you two what you wanted for breakfast?" Lou asked.

"Yes, she did. She's a nice lady."

"No, she's nicer than nice; she's a living saint, an angel sent straight from heaven."

"You're a lucky guy, Mr. Searing."

"You got that right! Help yourself to some coffee when it stops dripping. I'm going back to bed."

"Good idea."

Lou hesitated. "Want to bet on Higgins?" Lou asked holding up a dollar bill. "This bill says he never heads this way."

"You're on."

TWENTY-TWO

At 5:32 a.m. at his cabin on Sonoma Lake, Bernard Higgins' garage door opened and he backed out his BMW. Streaks of silver paint glistened along the passenger side of the dark blue vehicle. No one was present to see the markings and Bernard knew he was taking a risk in bringing the vehicle out and onto public roads, but he needed to complete his mission. He made his way to I-94 without attracting any attention.

As the BMW sped under the South Westnedge Exit overpass on I-94, a state trooper running a radar check noted that the vehicle was traveling over the speed limit. Also, the right rear brake light was non-functioning. Pursuing the vehicle, he was able to get the license number. When the computer showed the vehicle was registered to Bernard Higgins, he called for backup and continued to follow at a distance. Just past the 131 exit, the trooper flipped the switch that activated his siren and swirling red gumball. Bernard glanced in his rearview mirror to find the police vehicle rapidly closing in on him. He looked down at the speedometer — eighty-two mph. He braked and pulled over, his heart beating fast.

As an officer approached the door with a bright flashlight, Higgins rolled down the window. "Sorry, Officer."

"You're in a hurry, mister. Getting an early start on your day?"

"Early start — yes, sir," Bernard replied. "With little traffic and good conditions, I guess I let the speed get away from me."

"Where are you going?"

"I'm heading over to Grand Haven for a meeting."

"I see. May I see your license and registration?"

"Yes, sir." The driver took a wallet from his back pocket, pulled his license out of its sleeve, handed it to the trooper, and then fumbled in the glove compartment for the registration, which he handed to the trooper. "What did you clock me at?" he asked.

"Eighty-two, and your right rear taillight is out."

With Higgins' license and registration in hand, the trooper turned toward his cruiser. "I'll be back in a minute."

In the cruiser, the trooper entered the driver's name into the computer. The screen showed general information about Bernard Higgins, as well as a flag that the owner of the vehicle could be armed and dangerous. The trooper noted a suggestion that if the vehicle is apprehended, white streaks of paint could be on the passenger side. If so, the driver could be suspect of a vehicle accident near Alma, Michigan. He reached for his radio.

Within three minutes, two more dark blue state police cruisers pulled up, one in front of the suspect and one behind the trooper who had pulled over the car. The troopers got out of their vehicles and took positions behind and in front of the suspect's car ready to intervene if needed. Bernard looked around in surprise. This is a lot of man power for a speeding ticket, he thought.

The trooper approached the vehicle, "Mr. Higgins, please step out of the vehicle, close the door and face it with your hands on top of the car."

"This is ridiculous!" Bernard Higgins sputtered, stepping out of the car. "I've gone eighty many times and never been pulled over. You're going to extremes, Officer. This is embarrassing."

Bernard was frisked for weapons and asked to open his trunk. After a protest he did grudgingly, and one of the troopers checked the contents.

"Firearm deer season is four weeks off, Mr. Higgins. Looks like you're early unless you're driving to Wyoming or Montana."

"No sir, going to Grand Haven. I do some target-shooting on a farm near there."

"We're taking you to the county jail, Mr. Higgins."

"What for? I haven't done anything!"

"We'll start with speeding, then a broken taillight, then transferring loaded firearms in a vehicle, and we'll work up to intent to do bodily harm."

As Bernard Higgins was escorted into the backseat of the state police cruiser, he realized that, while he had a good lawyer, the next several years were as good as wasted.

Killing Lou and Jack would have to wait for another day. Today would be spent getting to know the men and women of the Battle Creek State Police Post, and some of Bernard's money would eventually go to support Michigan's officers-in-blue.

The Battle Creek State Police Post Commander passed along word to the Calhoun sheriff's department that Bernard Higgins had been picked up west of Kalamazoo for speeding. Weapons and plans to use them against Lou Searing and Jack Kelly had been found in his vehicle. The news was quickly relayed by cell phone to officer Northrup waiting in the Searing home in Grand Haven.

"No sense waking up our people," Northrup said to Cantrell. "They're safe now."

At 7:30, Jack, Elaine, and Carol were having breakfast when Lou walked from his bedroom through the living room. Officer Northrup hailed him. "You owe me that buck, Mr. Searing. Higgins was arrested west of Kalamazoo at 6:22 this morning."

"Got him, huh?" Lou remarked. "Good. I'll pay you after breakfast." He padded into the kitchen mumbling to himself.

As Lou poured syrup onto a neat stack of hotcakes, he said to Jack, "Guess we're close to wrapping up this case."

Carol kept the pancakes coming, the orange juice flowing, and crisp bacon on the griddle. The sun came up, the lake was calm, and they had another day to solve the murder of Janet Reid.

"I think we should get an early start — and obey the speed limit," Lou suggested. "We need to finish this before anyone else gets big ideas."

"I agree. Maybe we should also make sure we have our licenses and registrations," Jack offered, to another round of chuckles.

Lou called Sheriff Pritchard and thanked him for the protective efforts of the Ottawa County deputies. While on the phone, Lou made the obvious statement, "Sheriff, we're about as close to solving this as close-up photos of five backs of heads. Is there such a thing as a lineup with people's backs to the reviewer? That's what I need."

"You've got to be kidding."

"No, I'm not. If I had a photo of the backs of the heads of a half-dozen people, I could build a good case for the prosecutor. Jack and I have five or six suspects, each of whom, or in any combination, could be the murderer, but we need back-of-the-head shots. Can you get a court order requiring such photos?"

"The judge would laugh me out of the chamber, Lou."

"I'll go with you when you submit the request to explain why this is necessary."

"That's a good idea."

"We don't need a search warrant, because what we want isn't out of sight. Our evidence is the back of someone's head."

Sheriff Pritchard explained Lou's request to the county prosecutor. "Mr. Searing claims he can solve this murder if he gets photos of the backs of about six heads. Is there any precedent in law for a court order for such a thing?"

"I suppose any request can be made. The issue is whether you can convince a judge that it's necessary to take these photos."

"Lou Searing says he can be convincing."

"Then my advice is to complete the paperwork and take it and Mr. Searing to the judge. Hopefully, she'll see fit to grant your request."

That afternoon, armed with the paper work and accompanied by Lou Searing, Sheriff Pritchard stood before Judge Sue Beatty in her office in Marshall, the Calhoun County Seat.

"Your Honor, we request an order to take photos of the backs of the heads of seven people. Their names are: Bernard Higgins of Battle Creek, Michigan; Eric Swanson of Indianapolis, Indiana; Gerald Shanks of Alma, Michigan; William Dillon, also of Alma; Michael Mulligan of North Muskegon, Michigan; Donald Collins of

Port Huron, Michigan; and Suzanne Starmann of Grand Ledge, Michigan. I have with me Mr. Louis Searing, who is assisting us in the investigation of the murder of Dr. Janet Reid. He will explain why we need these photos."

Judge Beatty leaned forward. "I've been a judge for going on thirty years and I have never heard such a request. I hope there's a good reason for it."

"We believe the photos are necessary and warranted, Your Honor. Mr. Searing can explain."

The judge nodded. "Please proceed."

"Thank you, Your Honor," Lou began. "While investigating the murder of Dr. Reid, we located some video taken at the Battle Creek Balloon Festival just prior to the explosion which killed her. In the video, a person can be seen rising from the ground next to the wicker basket of Dr. Reid's balloon.

"At the state police lab in Lansing, the technician was able to discern that the person, man or woman, has a pierced left ear and that the right earlobe had recently undergone plastic surgery. There is also an indentation in the hair style indicating regular use of a cap or hat. We believe that if we have a photo of the back of the head of each of our suspects, we can match the video to the photo. Then Mr. Kelly and I believe we can build a case that will show beyond a reasonable doubt that whosever's head matches the video image is the killer."

"Thank you, Mr. Searing. Your reasoning is logical, and I don't see any reason why the photos shouldn't be taken," Judge Beatty stated with conviction. "I would ask that perhaps only one photo be taken at a time. Would this give you the information you need? I can't see inconveniencing seven people if your first photographic subject proves to be the match. Do you agree?"

"Yes, but I ask Your Honor to consider the possibility of word getting out that we are doing this. The surprise factor is important to getting spontaneous photos."

"I understand and I agree with you."

"Thank you, Your Honor," Lou said respectfully.

"I order that the photos be taken," Judge Beatty explained. "Legal counsel must be present, so each person is assured of his or her rights being upheld. That way, the police, or you, or I don't come under unwarranted criticism for our actions."

"I understand," Lou said.

"I'm signing the order at this time. Sheriff Pritchard, you may begin to collect these photos."

"Thank you, Your Honor."

As Lou left the courtroom he discovered he'd received a call from Carol.

"Lou, you got a call from a priest in Alma, a Father McDonald. He wants to talk with you about the Reid murder. He called Sheriff Pritchard, but the sheriff told him to call you as well."

"Okay. Did he leave a phone number?" Carol read off an Alma number.

"Okay thanks," Lou said. "I'll call him right away."

Father McDonald answered after three rings.

"Father, this is Lou Searing, returning your call."

"Yes, thank you, Mr. Searing. I've been troubled for many days. The stress is becoming quite difficult for me. I need to speak with you."

"Pardon me, but this is a switch, Father. Usually it's me talking to the priest, not the other way around."

Father failed to see the humor in Lou's comment. "I understand." Father McDonald took a deep breath. "A penitent came into the confessional about two weeks ago to confess a sin, and I absolved him of his sin, but before leaving this person said…"

"Stop, Father. Please," Lou begged. "As a Catholic I know you can't divulge anything you hear in confession. Whatever you say may help with this investigation, but keeping silent is important, so please don't say a word about this visit."

"I've been carrying this burden around for many days. When I learned of the murder of Dr. Reid, I almost became ill realizing that I may have been able to prevent this terrible event."

"I can imagine your pain, but keeping the confessional a place where a penitent is assured confidentiality is important to me and I know it is to you."

"Thank you, Mr. Searing."

Sheriff Pritchard decided he ought to handle this court order for photographs instead of delegating the job to his deputies. He contacted each person to be photographed, told them of the court order, and explained that he and a staff member would appear with the court order to take a photo of the back of each person's head. He advised the subjects that they should have legal counsel with them. He stated that the photo had to do with a criminal investigation. No one had been charged with a crime, but each photograph was needed by the investigators. The sheriff told each person he would call about fifteen minutes before his arrival. Sheriff Pritchard was somewhat surprised to find that people had no objection to the photos. Nobody complained or made light of the request.

The photographer was extremely careful not to misidentify anyone. Each photo was dated and the time of day was entered onto the photo. These were matched to a log so that a match could be made with minimal error.

Once the set of photos was compiled, they were sent electronically to the state police crime laboratory attention of Sergeant Smith. The Sergeant set about doing a simple match to the video, and within an hour he phoned Lou with his results.

"Do we have a match?" Lou asked anxiously.

"Yes, we do. The video image matches the photo for Eric Swanson."

"Okay. Is the match obvious."

"No question about it."

"Great; a few questions, please. Did this man have plastic surgery on his right earlobe?"

"That is unusual, Lou, but that would be my conclusion."

"Isn't that rare?"

"I've never heard of it before. Maybe he had a growth removed. He could have had an injury as a result of a fight or something, I suppose. But make no mistake: the two photos are Eric Swanson."

"He wears an earring in the left ear?"

"Maybe, but in both photos the piercing is there, but he has no earring in the lobe."

"Could that be the reason for the plastic surgery? Maybe he's closing them and chose to do the left before the right."

"That's highly unlikely. If you leave them alone for a few months, they close normally. You're the detective — you could just ask him."

"I know. I'm fixating on the lobes instead of getting on with your firm ID of the man at the festival as Eric Swanson. Thanks, Sergeant."

Lou called Jack. "Well, guess whose back-of-the-head matches the video at the festival?"

"What's behind door number two if I choose that one?" Jack asked.

"How about a new convertible?"

"Okay. I'll choose door number two and say the person is Bill Dillon."

"Nope, want to try door number one, or door number three?"

"I'll choose door number one and say, Bernard Higgins."

"Nope."

"Give me a break. My final guess is door number three and I'll say Eric Swanson."

"You win."

"I thought we were looking for a woman," Jack said. "But I do agree that you can't tell if the person is a man or woman in the video clip. But the specialist says the man in the photo is the balloonmeister, Eric Swanson."

"It makes perfect sense for the person to be Eric because the balloonmeister inspects the balloons," Lou stated. "That's his job. All of this back-of-the-head stuff is for naught. The guy was simply where he was supposed to be!"

"Yeah. But that doesn't mean he can't be a suspect," Jack replied.

"And, you'll recall that Eric had a motive — the book deal gone bad. And, you'll recall that Bernard Higgins knew him and Bernard Higgins had access to explosives."

"Very good, Lou! Very good!" Jack said, the light dawning in his mind. "No, I didn't pick up on that. How about the pierced left earlobe?"

"Guys with pierced ears are as common as gnats on a hot summer night."

"That's true. So, we have our murderer? Case closed?" Jack asked.

"We're on the right track, but I hardly think the case is closed."

"What's left to do?" Jack asked.

"Just placing someone at the basket of a balloon that explodes an hour later is not enough to convince a judge to send the case to trial, let alone convince a jury of guilt."

"What do we do next, then?" Jack asked.

"Well, we need to find a motive for Eric."

"He was getting revenge for his bad book deal," Jack replied.

"That's assumed, but we need proof, Jack."

"Okay, we need a motive. What else?"

"A big question is, did he act alone?" Lou said. "There are so many characters in this drama that we can't assume he acted alone, although he may have."

"A conspiracy?"

"Could be. Maybe he was paid to do this. Maybe the students asked him to kill Reid. There are a lot of questions."

"Sounds like you think we can't even be sure Eric killed Reid. Right?"

"Exactly! All we know for sure, if we believe Sergeant Smith, is that Eric was at the Balloon Festival, and he was by the wicker basket. End of what we know," Lou summarized.

"Okay, there's work to do," Jack replied.

"Yes, still plenty of work to do."

TWENTY-THREE

Later, Lou called Jack again "I have one more research question for you. I want to know if Eric Swanson is Catholic."

"Can I ask him?" Jack asked.

"I suppose so. I'd rather he not know it's me asking, but if that's the only way to find out, it'll have to do."

"Okay, give me his phone number." Lou did so.

Jack disconnected, then dialed the number.

"Hello, Mr. Swanson?"

"Yes?"

"I am calling on behalf of the pope's annual appeal. I thought you, as a practicing Catholic, might like to donate. Can I interest you in this worthwhile activity?"

"I'm afraid your calling list is in error. I'm not Catholic, although I'm sure your appeal is worthy."

"I'm sorry, sir. Thanks for talking to me. Goodbye."

Jack called Lou back. "Swanson's not Catholic."

"Boy, that was fast!"

"Your wish is my command, Lou. Anything else you need?"

"That's it, Jack. Thanks."

"But it isn't what you wanted to hear, is it?" Jack asked.

"You're right. Had he been Catholic, he could be the person Father McDonald mentioned who came to confession," Lou replied. "That, along with the revenge factor, and his being in the vicinity of the balloons at the festival would give us a tight case against him in Reid's murder."

"How about a meeting between Maggie, Heather, you and me?" Jack suggested.

"Great idea! A think-tank meeting just might put the pieces of the puzzle together."

"Good. I'll see if Maggie and Heather can come to our home, and I know you can come down, right?" Lou suggested.

"Absolutely; tell me when and I'll be there."

I'll contact you once I have a plan," Lou said.

Everyone could meet late the next afternoon. Each was to bring all their information and theories. Carol and Elaine offered to provide an easy dinner, in exchange for a game of Balderdash later in the evening.

After dinner, the four detectives gathered in the family room, with Samm snuggled by Lou's feet. Lou suggested, "Heather, since you are new to the team, why don't you begin? Who, to your way of thinking, is our murderer?"

"This is so exciting! I'm thrilled to be in the same room with the three of you. I feel like I'm playing the parlor game 'Clue', so I'll say, Mr. Higgins did it with a bomb at the balloon festival."

"That's a good beginning. On what evidence do you base this accusation?" Lou asked.

"Well, he seems to fit a lot of the criteria. He's Catholic, connected to Alma, has a nephew who was in Dr. Reid's class, and he himself suggested the students come up with alibis. And, the most telling evidence was his attempt, or at least his plan, to harm the two of you," Heather said, pointing to Lou and Jack.

Maggie added, "But a major factor is missing, Heather."

"I know, I know," Heather admitted. "He was in Kentucky. But, if you took his fingerprints, I'd bet my wheelchair that one would match the print on a piece of the bomb fragment."

"Maggie, what do you think?" Lou asked.

"My gut tells me that Bill Dillon is the killer. He is emotional, impulsive, and capable of aggression. He has a motive, in that he was furious with the college for the anguish his friend Al Nowak was being subjected to. Plus, I recall Lou mentioning that he learned about ballooning from Dr. Reid who gave him lessons a while ago."

"Problem: he may not be Catholic," Jack offered.

"We might agree with you, but we heard a different side of Bill Dillon from Becca Norris in the Advancement Office," Lou mused. "It sort of changed our minds about him as a suspect. But you're entitled to your opinion, and you could be right. We're not here to judge each other's thoughts, so thank you, Maggie. Your turn, Jack. Who is your murderer?"

"I'm going to throw a curve into this mess. For what it's worth, I think the president's husband is guilty."

"Really?" Lou said, surprised.

"I don't have much, if any, evidence, but I do know that President Shanks had a major headache with this professor. The root of the case is Dr. Reid, who brought dishonor to the campus and caused tremendous upsets by her behavior. The Board of Regents wasn't happy. The administrative staff was not happy. Parents were upset and students demoralized, all because of this visiting professor. Most of the president's problems disappeared when Dr. Reid died."

"But the president supported Dr. Reid — at least that's what we've been led to believe — she even suggested Reid become dean someday," Maggie offered.

"Yes, but why wouldn't a college president support a gifted chemist visiting her college? Why wouldn't a president want high standards?" Jack replied.

"Okay, my turn," Lou said, now reaping the benefit of his colleagues' thinking. "I have a combination for you to consider. The murderer is the balloonmeister, Eric Swanson. The motive is revenge for the injustice, apparently, of losing the book deal. The bomb was supplied by Bernard Higgins who had access to the necessary technology and explosives from his building contractor in Sturgis.

"Consider this scenario: Higgins probably learned of Swanson's book problems, and they might have conspired to kill Reid. Higgins comes to Alma to check on his nephew. Higgins thinks of Bert Dugan as a son. While in Alma, he goes to confession. Higgins urged his nephew Bert to have his friends fabricate alibis so they wouldn't be brought into the murder. He knows they didn't commit it because he did, but he didn't want them under constant scrutiny by the police and by us. In reality he wanted attention on the students and if one were caught telling a lie, he would be further removed from being involved. He has an alibi, in that he was in Kentucky, but all of his work was done on Friday: go to Alma; meet and strategize with Bert; go to confession; then pick up the bomb from his contractor in Sturgis and deliver it to Eric who was staying in Battle Creek before the festival. Suzanne is a no-brainer — innocent. The fire undoubtedly was an accident as the fire marshal determined."

"Very good, Lou," Jack offered, while Maggie and Heather nodded happily.

"And," Lou added, "I think Heather is absolutely correct. A fingerprint from Bernard Higgins will likely match the fingerprint on the bomb part and that will put him behind bars for a long time. Now, can anyone shoot down my theory or challenge it in any way?"

Maggie thought it through, as did Heather and Jack. Maggie spoke after a telling pause. "Based on all we have, I think Lou's theory is sound." The other two nodded agreement.

Jack, looking pensive, asked, "Lou, how do you explain Bernard Higgins forcing Dean Atkins off the road? Why was Dean Atkins a threat to Higgins?"

"I don't know. That will have to come out in court. My guess is that his nephew told him something that made Atkins a threat. Good question, Jack, but I don't know."

"We know the police checked the paint scrapings on Higgins' and Atkins' cars, and the car that hit Atkins was definitely registered to Higgins," Jack summarized. "But maybe Higgins wasn't driving the car. Maybe Bert Dugan had borrowed his uncle's car and drove Atkins off the road."

"I'm leaving that crime up to whoever has jurisdiction. It's enough for us to bring closure to the fire and murder. But I applaud you, Jack, for your thinking. Maybe it wasn't Higgins who forced him off the road. I jumped to that conclusion which I should not have done!"

TWENTY-FOUR

October 26

Early the next morning, Lou called Sheriff Pritchard and Deputy Jaggers and spent quite a while reviewing the conclusions the group had reached the evening before. Lou's account made sense. Armed with his theory, Sheriff Pritchard and Deputy Jaggers obtained a warrant for the arrest of Bernard Higgins. Because he was already in custody, the arrest involved nothing other than contacting him, reading him his Miranda rights, and making sure he had an attorney.

A search of the Higgins home revealed damaging evidence. His computer contained numerous messages to his nephew Bert Dugan, the most recent saying, "Bert, you may be hearing news about Searing and Kelly. They are closing in on me and they need to be taken out. Uncle Bernie."

Deputy Jaggers had driven to Indianapolis. He and Indianapolis police officers knocked on Eric Swanson's door. He opened it cautiously fearing he was to hear news of a death in his family, but he quickly learned that the officers had a warrant for his arrest for the murder of Janet Reid. Eric didn't resist. He waived extradition. As police searched the entryway of his home in northeast Indianapolis, they noticed a colorful tam o'shanter on a hook. "Are ye ah Scotsman?" one of the officers asked with a Scottish brogue.

Eric simply nodded, and then slightly shook his head in painful recognition that his life was forever changed.

After the two arrests were made and charges filed, Sheriff Pritchard called Lou with the news. "We've worked with the Indiana authorities to have Swanson brought up here and that will finalize this thing. Then the prosecutor and the justice system take over. You and Jack have solved another one, Lou. I can't thank you enough."

"Just lucky, Sheriff."

"Forget that humble line, Lou. It wasn't luck, it was good detective work, and you and Jack deserve all the credit. Bert Dugan cooperated and we were able to nip his uncle's murder plan in the bud."

"Yes, Bert's e-mail was key to solving this case. Jack and I appreciate his kindness."

"Bert told me he liked and respected you, and while he respected his uncle for all he had done for him, he came to see you as more of a father figure in recent days. He couldn't bear the thought of anything happening to you or to Jack."

"He's a fine young man. Actually, he's typical of an Alma student — conscientious, compassionate, and willing to do what is right."

"I'll let you tell President Shanks and Dean Atkins of the arrests. Normally I would, or I'd ask Chief Worthington to do it. But you've worked with the college for almost a month, and I think the news should come from you. Chief Worthington knows of the arrests and he agreed I should ask you to inform the college administrators."

"It is always a joy to give someone good news. And I can assure you, their hearing that the case is closed will be like seeing fresh heather blooming at Loch Lomond in the springtime."

Prior to calling President Shanks, Lou contacted Dean Atkins, who was still in the hospital, to tell him that Bernard Higgins' vehicle had forced him off the road, but he couldn't verify that Bernard was driving. "Oh, yes. I've had many calls from him. Talk about an angry man. You've heard of 'stage moms'? Well, this is a 'college dad' — okay, uncle — who had to challenge everything. I mean, it seems I got a call if he found out Bert didn't like the mashed potatoes. I'm exaggerating, but you know what I mean."

"Very difficult guy," Lou replied. "We don't know why he considered you a threat, but he'll be punished for his actions.

Upon hearing the news of the arrests, President Shanks thanked Lou. "What pleases me most, and I know Dean Atkins will agree, is that even with the heartache this has brought to Alma College, I'm relieved that not one person at our college was involved in crime. We went through a lot — the students, faculty, alumni, parents. But the fire was an accident, and our visiting professor was murdered by a person connected with an outside interest. We can now begin healing and put our energy into the business of educating some of our nations' finest young people, unclouded by fear."

As President Shanks spoke, Lou heard some music in the background. "What do I hear?"

"Oh, it's a warm day, and my window is open a little, so I can hear the Kiltie Band practicing on the football field. What you hear is the alma mater, Lou." President Shanks said, "You'll remember this Lou. Your mother played it on the piano on this campus, and I imagine you sang it while you were here."

President Shanks put the phone near the open window, and Lou could hear the music. Memories of long ago came into his mind as he imagined his mother as a youthful coed and gifted pianist, playing and singing, "Loyal hearts will cherish ever, thoughts of thee throughout the years. Pledging thee a fond devotion, guardian of our hopes and fears. Alma, Alma, sing of alma mater; thy loyal children chant thy hymn of praise."

A week later at a convocation before the student body and faculty, Lou, Jack Kelly, Maggie, and Heather received certificates of appreciation from President Shanks. "On behalf of the faculty, students, and alumni of Alma College, I thank Mr. Searing, Mr. Kelly, Mrs. McMillan, and Ms. Moore for resolving this tragic chapter in our history. Let's now begin to heal and enjoy the benefits of the liberal arts college experience."

The tributes continued to come, this time to Heather Moore. At an assembly at Battle Creek Central High School, Heather was honored for her part in helping to solve the murder of Janet Reid. She and all the students enjoyed a visit from Tony the Tiger from the Kellogg Company who awarded Heather a full scholarship to Alma College from the Kellogg Foundation. The mayor of Battle Creek presented her with a key to the city. And Director John Ickes, from the Hot Air Balloon Festival, gave Heather and her family a lifetime pass to the festival. He also announced that Heather would be Grand Marshall of the 2009 Hot Air Balloon Festival Parade.

EPILOGUE

Bernard Higgins and Eric Swanson were tried and convicted of the murder of Janet Reid. Both are serving life terms in a men's correctional facility in Ionia. The magnificent book on ballooning was never published.

Bill Dillon participated in anger-management classes and will graduate from Alma in June.

Don Collins transferred to St. Clair Community College.

Mr Mulligan was relieved that the fire was an accident and not the result of advice he had given Don Collins.

Ten of the eleven registered students in Chem 231 are continuing their education at Alma College. Each is expected to maintain a high GPA, allowing him or her to apply to graduate schools of their choosing.

Suzanne Starmann dropped out of Alma. She continues to receive therapy while appearing in Grand Ledge theatrical productions.

Al Nowak remains a student at Alma and is an active member of Tau Kappa Epsilon. He has changed his major from pre-theology to pre-law.

President Elizabeth Shanks continues to lead Alma College in its pursuit of excellence.

Gerald Shanks was surprised to learn that he was suspect. Being the husband of a college president is a unique experience, but he never dreamed he could be considered a possible murderer.

Dean Atkins regained his health and returned as Dean of Students. He is enjoying a less stressful semester.

Maggie McMillan and Heather Moore enjoyed helping Lou and Jack and hope to be involved in the next investigation.

Elaine Kelly after she calmed down a bit, acknowledged Jack's talents. Jack will continue to assist whenever Lou needs his trusted ally.

Lou and Carol Searing enjoy their home south of Grand Haven on the shore of Lake Michigan. They look forward to their beloved evening walks with Samm next spring. Warmer weather can't come soon enough for them, nor for Millie, who perhaps looks forward to napping on the porch.

And yes, Lou and Jack rode in a hot air balloon, compliments of John Ickes and the Battle Creek Balloon Festival. Carol and Elaine watched from the ground as the two men enjoyed the peaceful glide above beautiful west Michigan.

THE END